prize
fighter

prize fighter

Sometimes the greatest
battle you can have
is with your past

FUTURE D. FIDEL

hachette
AUSTRALIA

hachette
AUSTRALIA

Published in Australia and New Zealand in 2018
by Hachette Australia
(an imprint of Hachette Australia Pty Limited)
Level 17, 207 Kent Street, Sydney NSW 2000
www.hachette.com.au

A catalogue record for this
book is available from the
National Library of Australia

978 0 7336 3905 0 (pbk.)

Cover design by Christabella Designs
Author photograph by Dylan Evans
Typeset in Adobe Garamond Pro by Kirby Jones
Printed and bound in Australia by McPherson's Printing Group

MIX
Paper from
responsible sources
FSC® C001695

The paper this book is printed on is certified against the Forest Stewardship Council® Standards. McPherson's Printing Group holds FSC® chain of custody certification SA-COC-005379. FSC®. promotes environmentally responsible, socially beneficial and economically viable management of the world's forests.

This book is dedicated to my beloved sister
Okanya Safi. My second mother who gave me
a second chance at this life.

She is the reason why this book has
seen the light.

contents

There is no easy walk to freedom anywhere, and many of us will have to pass through the valley of the shadow of death again and again before we reach the mountaintop of our desires.

NELSON MANDELA

ACT I

chapter 1

the alakis

My name is Isa Alaki.

I am not from here.

I'm originally from a small village called Kazimia, on the coast of Lake Tanganyika, which sits below a vastly stretched mountain in the Democratic Republic of the Congo (the DRC). I was born in Kazimia and know all about the places around it. Kavumbwe is found towards the southern side of my village, and if you continue further south by boat you can reach Kalemie. Travelling the other way, to the north from my birth village, you will find Kalamba, and further in that direction is Ubwari, Baraka and Uvira.

If you head to the west, you will arrive in Kikonde, a small village of approximately ten thousand people, mostly farmers, where my parents are from. My forefathers arrived in Kikonde to farm cassava, rice, palm oil and sugarcane, and it was here that my father was born. He was named after his great-grandfather, Alaki Ombele. Alaki, meaning 'promise', and Ombele, meaning 'ahead'. My beloved mother's name was Patience. She was not always as her name suggests.

We are from the Bembe tribe: a very tough and proudly complicated tribe with vast knowledge. In our tradition, when you present yourself in a group of other tribes, you begin your introduction with: *I am mshi ...* – meaning, 'I belong to' – then you call the name of your tribe. If you're more than one person, you would say, *We are bashi ...*

Bembe – or Babembe – have many clans, which are grouped from the immediate family to extended families of approximately ten generations. A clan is named according to its forefathers' beliefs or relationship to nature. Sometimes they're named after their greatest warriors or leaders. For example, there's *Bashi-m'nyaka* – the Wind Clan; *Bashi-N'gyoku* – the Elephant Clan; *Bashi-Nyange* – named for Nyange, a great Bembe leader; and so on. I am *Mshi-N'gyoku*. My parents lived in Kazimia because clans stay close to each other, unless someone decides to leave for another place, ready to start the Bembe tribe elsewhere. My father decided to do this, and so we moved to Bukavu when I was five years old.

My friends in Kazimia were from my tribe, so we spoke the same language. Each day after school I played marbles with my friends Toni, Écasa and Amishi, or sometimes we played soccer using beer-bottle lids mixed with Fanta-bottle lids as players, with a small black ball called *asolô* as a soccer ball. As posts, we used two batteries and another one in the middle as a goalkeeper. Sometimes, in the moonlight, we played hide and seek with the girls, when they were done playing rope swing or double-dutch. In my language, we call it *beyâ*. Their favourite game was *horo*. It's like double-dutch, but they used a small ball. The two people on the outside have to try and hit the one in the middle with the ball. The longer someone can stay in the middle, the more fun they would have.

From our village we could see smoke rising from the mountains before the sunset. The clan there, the *Bafuliru*, often burned the entire bushland in order to hunt for small animals like *seyâ* and *sengi,* which look like rats only bigger; one *seyâ* can feed an entire family for at least three days. Because these animals reside close to rivers, hunters would set the bushland on fire then wait by the river. Animals run to the river to escape the flames, but when they get there they can't swim and they are caught between the water and the fire. The *Banyamulenge*, who also lived in the mountains, were mostly unhappy when the bushlands were burnt because they used it to feed their cattle. My father told me that the *Banyamulenge* came to the DRC as refugees from Rwanda in the early 60s. They now live in the mountains like Congolese.

Curiosity makes my people strive for other places and other things, and so they are inherently itinerant, always looking for a better life. My ancestors, originally from Togo, descended as nomads down the coast of Africa and have now spread across many other countries. Everywhere they resided, they fought for freedom as citizens of that country. Togo has many of my tribe. You can also find my people in Congo-Brazzaville, Malawi, Zimbabwe, South Africa, Angola, Cameroon, Uganda, South Sudan, Kenya, Burundi and Tanzania. I know our history very well, because my father made sure my brother, my sister and I know our people. Know our strengths.

Tanzania is a country in the east, across Lake Tanganyika. The closest Tanzanian town from where I lived as a child is Kigoma, and it is where most of my tribe living in Tanzania still reside. At night when the moon didn't shine, I could see the streetlights blazing across the water from Kigoma. Sometimes the lights from fishing boats would deceive me, but I could tell that they weren't streetlights when I saw them moving across the lake. Streetlights don't move.

My brother, Moïse, wanted to be a fisherman, but he was never good at catching big fish. Whenever he fished he would mostly catch tilapia, which are small. I love the big fish, though. *Nonzi* is the biggest fish you can catch in Lake Tanganyika. Moïse never caught any *nonzi*, so my father would always buy them from other fisherman. I love *ndûbó* – or, as I like to call it, the zebra rhino fish. It has black and white stripes like a zebra with a big horn on its forehead like a rhinoceros. Sometimes, when it gets bigger, the white stripes turn to light blue. It's my favourite fish, but I also like to eat *nkengê*, the only fish caught at night. It has good meat and tastes like barramundi. I am scared of *ni'â* – it's a small fish but very dangerous. It can electrocute you, and if you are in a canoe when you catch it you could fall in the water and become a crocodile's meal. There are a lot of crocodiles in the lake. They hide under the rocks when they want to attack you. Sometimes they pretend to be a floating branch to trick you into feeling safe and then they catch you with their sharp teeth.

Our house in Kazimia was a two-bedroom mud structure with a grass-thatched roof. I was the youngest child and I shared a room with Moïse while my sister slept in the other bedroom with Mama and Papa. Our kitchen was in a different, smaller house on the opposite side of the main house, and inside it was a stove made of three rocks placed on the ground like a triangle. My sister would gather firewood when they went farming, and my mother would arrange the firewood between the rocks and then place a pan on top of the rocks to cook *ugali*. *Ugali* is our traditional food. My parents told me that every African child is brought up on its deliciousness. It is a meal prepared using maize flour or semolina. My mother mixed the flour in boiling water over the fire, stirring until it was ready. We would then eat it with soup. I loved having *ugali* with roasted fish, especially *ndûbó*. When it came to roasting *ndûbó*, my mother would wait until the fire had burned down to coals because it is a special fish and it doesn't taste good smoked.

In Kazimia I would carry a basket and follow my sister, Rita, every time she went to the forest to find mushrooms. We would leave home at 2pm and search until it was dark. The biggest mushroom we could find was the taka. I wasn't able to carry it alone, so my sister would carry it.

After we brought the mushrooms home, I would go with my sister to fetch water. The creek was two kilometres away from our house, and my sister was scared to go alone because it was near the cemetery. My brother didn't want to take her because he was always too busy showing off to girls with his slingshot, so I would go with Rita.

I think that's why my father brought us to Bukavu. He wanted us to study and have a better life than he had. In our new, larger house I had my own room, where I could sleep without being disturbed by my brother. This house was built on concrete, with cement floors and paintings on the walls. The outer walls were covered in rough cement, and the metal tiles on the roof were far better than the grass roof we were used to. We had a huge balcony looking out across the front yard, where square tiles covered the fence which ran all the way to the main road then surrounded the entire house. A metal gate let us in and out. And the backyard was filled with my mother's garden. My sister and I helped her plant pineapples, passionfruit and avocado trees. When the fruit ripened we would take some to school and my mother would give some to our neighbours or to fellow churchgoers.

My whole extended family grew up in a Christian church. The name Isa is translated to my native language Bembe from the Biblical name Isaac. Our church, Association Ministaire Biblique (AMB), is one of the biggest churches in our region, after the Catholic and Methodist churches. Every week after Sunday school we would wait for the adults to come to church just to listen to the choir. They would sing beautiful melodies following the lead of a solo guitar that played a Congolese rhythm.

During the week I went to school, and when it all happened I was in grade four. I loved studying because I wanted to build bridges when I grew up. Our school was located on the other side of Bukavu, at the bottom of a small hill. It was a twenty-minute walk from my house, and on the way we had to cross the Ruzizi River, which flows along the edge of the border with Rwanda.

When we first moved to Bukavu I only spoke Kibembe and Swahili, but I soon started to pick up Lingala, and my teacher, Mr Tambu, also taught me French. He told me every Congolese had to know the national language, but French is very complicated, and I preferred to study maths. I'm very good at solving complex equations.

I wanted to grow up to be like my father. I wanted to wake up at six o'clock every morning to the sound of an alarm for a very important job. But I wanted to do something different from what he did. I wanted to be an engineer. I was going to build bridges. I'd put on my black trousers and white shirt with a grey tie like my father, briefcase in my hand and off I'd go to work to design bridges and tall storage buildings like the one across the road from our house. My father was pleased that I wanted to build bridges. He told me I would go to study in Kigali when I was older. But after the great genocide he changed his mind and decided he would send me to Belgium instead.

Every now and then, my father used to take me to his office after school. He loved his job the same way he loved us. His three children. Especially me. He loved me the most because I'm special. That's what he told me every morning. He said, 'You're my last born, that's what makes you special.' My father gave me anything I desired, and he watched over me. He protected me. I also knew I was special because his office desk was decorated with pictures of me: when I was a year old, another when I was three years old, and a picture he took of me with my brother on Moïse's fifteenth birthday. My father would tell me I had to study and work hard in school if I wanted to be like him, and that was what I was going to do.

Just like my brother and sister, I was proud to carry the Alaki name, my father's name, because he was a respected man in Bukavu and in his clan. Every man and woman listened to him when he spoke.

My mother, Patience, would take my father's briefcase when he came home from work very tired. She was the queen of the house. She wanted everything done as soon as she said so, otherwise someone would be belted. Since I was the youngest, blame would always fall on me if something went wrong in the house. I tried to blame everything on my sister, Rita. I wanted to see her take the beatings because she was always picking on me. She was treated differently because she was a girl. 'Mum, I'm sick,' and she would be allowed to skip school. 'Dad, I'm hungry,' and she could eat whatever she wanted. 'Dad, Isa is laughing at me,' and I was sent to my room. Even though I was my father's favourite she could make him punish me. She was such a drama queen! She was very good at sport, though. Rita came second in her running carnival, and before it all happened she went to Goma to race against students from other schools.

Moïse was a charmer. Tall and handsome; at least he thought so. But I didn't think he was. He was too big for his age and always carried around the slingshot Dad bought for him. He could talk to any girl he wanted, and it seemed he was talking to a different girl every time I saw him. At soccer training or whenever we went bird hunting, he'd always end up talking to some girl, even though I knew he liked one in particular: Anna.

Anna lived two blocks away from our house in Bukavu. Moïse was always taking me to her house whenever her parents were away farming. At a certain point he would tell me to turn around and close my eyes. One day I accidentally opened them before he told me to, and I saw him biting Anna's lips. I asked him why but he never would tell me. Back then I thought that Anna must have hidden lollies in her mouth.

Fridays in Bukavu meant soccer games. One particular night when I was nine years old, all the big boys from our school were playing against the boys from Garderi, a school across town. I went to support Moïse; I supported him in everything, even when he wouldn't tell me why he bit Anna. That night Rita was away, so instead of walking home with her I had to wait for Moïse. He took a long time after the game to come out and find me.

When we got home, I was hungry and tired. I opened the front door and could smell my favourite dish of cooked antelope meat with rice. I love rice and I love meat. My stomach started rumbling before I even opened the pot. To me this was welcoming, heavenly food. The table was set and there was a bundle of flowers close to the plates and a card next to one that said *Joyeux anniversaire*. A card like this was rare in Bukavu, so it must have been ordered from Goma. Everything was placed in the middle of a heart symbol made from individual chocolates. I love chocolates too, even more than meat and rice.

My father was in the bathroom. I could hear the echo as he whistled to his favourite song and the splash of water on the floor. I stood looking at those chocolates, thinking to myself, *I am hungry and I just came from school, then soccer games. Watching a soccer game is very tiring. That should be a good excuse to take one piece of meat, one scoop of rice, and just one chocolate.* I took the first scoop, and that was my mistake. I couldn't stop. After a few minutes, I heard my father's footsteps approaching the living room, so I put the last chocolate in my mouth and quickly hid under the dining table.

'What happened to the food I left on the table?' my father shouted.

'I didn't do it!' I mumbled with my full mouth from under the table. I knew my miserable lie would lead me to my mother's belt.

My mother always told me not to lie, and she made us go to church every Sunday morning. I loved listening to the choir as they sang. The melody of the song mixing with the lead guitar would stay in my head the whole week. Mum said I had to be a good boy and pray every night before bed and every morning when I woke. She taught me how to pray before my meal and told me I should always love and respect others. She also told me I would face her belt if I ever lied. Each time I was punished she would make me lie face down, though when she was really angry she wouldn't give me time and she would give me a beating standing up. She was unpredictable. As I came out from under the table only one thing was running through my mind: 'Am I going to be able to sit down after this?'

The next day, I was woken up by my dad's 6am alarm. He opened my bedroom door and said, 'Isa, you're coming with me today.' It was the best news I'd heard in years. The only thing that soured the moment was the fact that my butt still burned from the belt. I knew clothes would make it feel worse, but I couldn't leave the house naked.

We drove down the streets to my father's office, where he worked with two other men and a woman. He was concentrating to steer away from any deep potholes, but everyone on the street seemed excited to see him. He greeted them with a smile.

Jambo!

He waved at everyone as we drove past our local supermarket. As motorbikes and cars passed, I heard them beep their horns as he pulled into the parking lot outside the six-door building where he worked. The office was built on a thick foundation of yellowish baked bricks. I stood close to them and they still smelled earthy and they were hot, as though storing the heat of the previous day. We were the first to arrive at the office. I loved to look at the fine paintings that covered the walls. A picture of the first Prime Minister, Patrice Émery Lumumba, was suspended above a desk across the room. This was my father's desk. Three more desks stretched across the opposite wall, side by side. My father sat me down at one of the desks and said, 'Here! Sort these papers out.'

As soon as I started my work, two men walked into the office wearing similar attire to my dad but they showed him respect, as if he were senior to them. I watched them go to their desks for a moment and then looked back at my own special task. There were many papers to sort and they all had the same heading, *Le mouvement du changement de la RD Congo* (The Movement of Change in DR Congo). My father didn't explain what these papers were for or what his job actually was. He always told me that I was still too young to understand, but that one day I would know how important it was.

As I sorted the papers I couldn't stop thinking about what I was going to tell all my friends at school about my new office job. All I needed was a clean shirt, clean trousers, some leather shoes and a tie to fit in.

Two hours later, my father had a visitor. His friend Zeze was a tall man who looked like he hadn't had anything to eat for weeks. He often came to our house to see how we were going, and he was a big supporter of my father. His family had been massacred in Rwanda during the genocide, so he lived alone. Dad had told me that Zeze was the

Army General in South Kivu, and today he arrived in his government uniform with his rankings on his shoulders.

I pretended I was concentrating but I listened hard to hear the conversation.

'You're doing a great job, my friend. Your movement is changing the people,' Zeze said. 'But we need to expand across the country. The people are ready. Otherwise, our neighbours and the West will plunder our resources and we will suffer.'

My father said something, but too softly for me to hear. His face was calm throughout but Zeze looked worried and he raised his voice slightly. 'There's steam coming from Rwanda, my friend, I would ask for you to be more vigilant because I'm being reassigned to Misisi. Maybe while I'm settled there, you can come talk to some people?' Zeze said.

'If there's steam coming, then why are you leaving?' my father asked.

'That, my friend, I don't know,' Zeze replied.

'Who's going to look after the people while you're gone?' my father said.

'Once again, that's a question I cannot answer. However, the good news is that Colonel Dunia is in Goma. People should be safe,' Zeze added.

'People would be safe if he was here, not hundreds of kilometres away.'

I tried to hear the rest but they lowered their voices. I looked over at the two other men in the office and they seemed to be listening too.

My father stopped talking and walked over to me with a sign that he picked up from against the wall. It said, 'Vote 1, Alaki Ombele'.

'Come with me Isa,' he said. And we all walked out to the car.

Zeze got into the driver's seat, my father into the passenger seat and I sat in the back with two of Zeze's soldiers, who had been waiting outside in the street. I didn't say a word as I watched people stare back at us as we drove to the city centre. There were many people gathered there, and I hung back as my father and Zeze walked to the front of the crowd and both spoke before many cameras and microphones. My father was running to become the governor of the district.

I was very proud of my father and couldn't wait to see him on TV that night, and to tell my friends I was there and saw the reporters record my father's interview. I was very proud to be my father's son, very proud to be an Alaki.

At home, after dinner, my father came on the evening news. My mother's eyes were filled with pride, Rita started crying and even Moïse, who often fought with my father, was impressed. My mother told me that my father would stop all the wars in the region and because of him we would all be safe. I believed her.

chapter 2

my brother held my hand

LIKE EVERY CHILD IN TOWN, I WOULD WAKE UP EACH morning for school and go to my lessons. It is the same in many places around the world. And, like many other children, once school was over we would gather to play games before we went home. It was always much the same, unless Moïse had different plans for me.

My fifteen-year-old brother Moïse didn't play around after school. He was focused on different things. And one of them was boxing. That was what he did every day after school, except for Fridays when he played soccer.

Sometimes I would go with Moïse to watch him train. The echo coming from the punching bag would hit my ears at high speed. The heavy bag was suspended in the middle of the room and it swung from side to side with each of my brother's hard hits. The heat from the frantic movement of bodies stirred the air and made the smell of sweat almost sweet; at times I felt I could taste it. I would sit in the corner and watch Moïse and other men he knew move and jab at each other or into the air. The floor was covered in rubber mats laid down in groups of four different colours: yellow, blue, red and orange. A big mirror covered a third of the right-side wall, and the rest of the walls were painted with pictures of boxers. All different types of boxers. Some were black, some Asian, others were white.

Moïse would always hang his shirt and slingshot on the same hook. I would watch the flash of reflections in the mirror and count the rotations of the jump rope when Moïse moved on from the bag. But always I would glance back to that slingshot. I wanted it to be mine but wouldn't dare touch it because I knew my brother would be angry.

I remember this day the most because of what happened soon after. Moïse was in front of the punching bag, hitting it over and over. It was his second bag. The first one was already on the floor leaking sand. I could hear him counting softly as he hit the bag, *one-two* over and over again. Sometimes he counted to four but never to five. A man stood behind Moïse instructing him to do things better. He was bigger than my brother. Built, too. Moïse told me he was the best coach because he started fighting when he was still a little boy. Moïse told me that because he wanted me to stop messing around and get serious about fighting.

I was exhausted just watching and wished I was back playing with my friends, but I knew better than to complain.

Moïse didn't fall into my traps easily. As an older brother, he was always the boss. But I knew he was there to protect me. He was a fighter. After watching a video tape of the legendary fight between Muhammad Ali and George Foreman, he had decided he would be a champion. And I had to admit, he acted like one. He spent all his time training, punching bullies and talking to girls.

I wanted to be like Moïse. With muscles bigger than his. My brother tried to teach me everything about fighting when we were on the streets. He always told me to protect myself, but I had him, so I never found it necessary. Back then, anyway. Back then he could protect me.

The week before it all happened, Moïse talked me into boxing against a boy at school. We were still in the playground and my schoolmates formed a circle, with us in the middle, so we could box like champions. Moïse was cheering and leading me on.

'You gotta kill this kid,' he said.

I didn't want to kill him, he was my friend.

'Don't be a coward!' Moïse shouted.

I landed a few punches, and it felt really good. I could see I had hurt my friend but I didn't care because Moïse cheered, and so I threw a few more punches. I hit hard.

I don't know how long we would have fought for but we were stopped by our teacher, who forced us to go home.

My brother held my hand proudly as we ran to his training gym.

This was the day my brother gave me my first proper boxing lesson. 'Jab, jab, duck!' he said. 'Stand up straight! Bend your knees a little bit; your back straight, head up, your left hand here, your right hand here. Jab, jab, duck!'

Moïse was fast, like the wind. His posture was carefully measured, like an attacking lion. I couldn't do things the way my brother could, but he told me to keep trying.

'You're going to need to learn. I won't always be here to protect you, and you will be facing much bigger enemies than me. Now try again.'

My body wanted to try but my mind wanted his slingshot. I wanted to have the vision of an owl, the strength of a lion and the speed of a cheetah. I knew I had to work harder, become fitter. My feet were still too heavy. The man who trained Moïse watched us both and said only this to me, 'Patience to keep trying is the beginning of success.'

After what seemed like endless training, Moïse agreed to take me hunting. We went home and told my mother we would not be back until late at night. My father was not at home to say no. I hoped Moïse would let me use his slingshot as a reward for punching hard and true.

He was going to teach me how to kill a bird. There are a number of ways. First, we used a thin stick stripped from the back of a palm tree's leaf and bent it into a small circular trap tightened with fishing line into a noose. We found a nest and put pawpaw under it. Some birds love pawpaw and when they try to eat this pawpaw, we catch them by the neck. I left my first trap on top of a tree, and waited. I had a basket of rocks balanced on top of my head and after a while, the pressure burned my neck. Moïse used his slingshot to kill pigeons. It worked better than the palm-frond noose. No matter how many times I asked to use his slingshot, Moïse said no. He always told me the same thing: 'You do not know how to aim! You must have a good eye to kill a bird!'

That made me cross. Moïse always thought he knew better, but he didn't. I said to him, 'I can understand what you mean by having a good eye with all of these birds we've already killed.' I waved an arm at the bare earth.

Moïse's eyes went small and his voice cold. 'We'll kill one, just wait!'

'That's all we do,' I said. 'Wait. I'm starting to think your smell is making them fly away before we get any closer. You stink like a wet dog.'

'Hah! Is it my smell, or those shorts you're wearing?' he mocked, the laughter back in his throat.

'These are my favourite shorts!'

'Why? Because they're big like your forehead?'

'I'll tell Dad you were talking about my forehead again!'

'You wouldn't dare!'

'Let me have a shot, then.'

By evening we still hadn't killed a bird. My feet were about to explode but Moïse didn't want to stop walking. I tried to distract him.

'Moïse, look at my biceps! They're getting big.'

Moïse laughed and told me I needed to do ten push-ups every morning, afternoon and night to even come close to his.

He didn't slow his pace, walking a step in front of me. And then he stopped suddenly. 'There's a girl coming, Isa. Start crying!'

I didn't ask why, I did what my brother told me.

'Excuse me, lady, can I have a piece of sugarcane for my brother? He's hungry.'

The girl pulled a piece of sugarcane from the basket she was carrying and handed it to me, telling me not to cry.

'You're very kind,' Moïse said, seeming to grow taller as he spoke. 'You go to my school, don't you?'

I stood chewing on the sugarcane as Moïse spoke to the girl. She smiled back at him. I just wanted to get home. I'd had enough of hunting and lessons on how to talk to a girl.

Before I had sucked all the goodness out of the cane, he said goodbye and watched as the girl walked away down the track. She glanced back and waved.

'Watch and learn Isa,' my brother told me. 'Only, remember one thing: don't ever try to impress people who don't matter to you. At the end of the day, they'll go unimpressed.'

I FELT GOOD that day. I felt like my brother and I were strong and that good things would come. I was wrong. My wary mother always kept an eye on Moïse and me. That night she noticed the lump on my forehead from my school boxing championship.

'How can you let your brother fight?' she screamed at Moïse. 'I told you to look after him.'

'I'm preparing him for danger,' Moïse said. 'You know these times are dangerous.'

As my mother and brother argued, my father walked in the door. He did not even take the time to put down his briefcase as he stepped between them. 'What did I tell you boys about fighting?' he said. His voice was gruff and his eyes sparked with anger.

'You've always told us to face our problems,' Moïse said.

'Not through violence. You don't solve things with your fist. You use your mind. That's why I sent you to school. Not to knock other children's heads together. You're an Alaki, Moïse, we don't fight with fists.'

Their argument went on, and this one was different to the arguments they'd had before.

'You're going to stay with your uncle in Goma,' my father said.

'No way! Uncle doesn't like me. I'm not going!' Moïse shouted.

My father ignored his words. 'I've spoken with your mother, and that is it! I have enrolled you into university there.'

'All you ever do is make decisions for others. You've never cared about what they want.' Moïse stood and moved towards my father, but my father was not afraid of him.

'This is for your own good, I need to protect you,' my father said.

Moïse kept arguing, telling my father, 'I have to stay. There's no one else who can protect the family, Dad. I will stay and I will fight!'

'You're going to Goma, and that is it.'

Later that night, I lay in bed and listened to Moïse stomp around the house and the murmurs of my mother and father from their room. I listened to the sounds outside. The crickets and night birds calling. It took a long time for sleep to find me.

chapter 3

the quickest legs, the fastest bullet

IT WAS A TUESDAY WHEN MOÏSE LEFT FOR GOMA. He
had argued right up until the moment my father put him
on the bus. I was sad to see him go and wanted to cry
as I said goodbye. But the sadness lifted when I saw what
Moïse had left for me on my bed. His slingshot.

I thought when Moïse was gone that calm would settle
on our house. But at dinner that night, my father looked
more furious than ever. My mother wasn't happy with my
father, and she told him so. She wanted us all to leave with
Moïse. My father told her he needed to stay and protect
the country. He said there were thieves and bad people
wanting to take what belonged to the Congolese people.
He saw my worried face and the look in Rita's eyes, and he
smiled. 'It will all be over very soon,' he told us. 'It will all
be okay.'

Rita and I went to bed that night and I lay there listening to the sound of my parents' voices through the wall. They were still arguing. I felt the air change. As the sun went to sleep the town grew silent, like a ghost town. It felt like something was coming.

The next morning was still too quiet. No roosters crowed an alarm; everyone had roasted theirs over the last few days to stop them becoming the rebel soldiers' next meal. The morning was heavy with smoke, making me feel breathless. My father left for work and I followed him out the door to go to school. Rita was staying home. I heard my mother say she was sick, but I think she was just sad.

That day was unlike any other and marked the beginning of the many horrors to come. As soon as I got to school a teacher started asking me about my father's job. I didn't know why. I headed to French class, and there my teacher, Mr Tambu, asked us all about who we wanted to become when we grew up. Aisha, who sat in front of me, told us she wanted to become a tailor.

I didn't get a chance to tell Mr Tambu that I wanted to wear a white shirt, pants and a tie and be like my father because the sound of gunshots and explosions rumbled down from the heavens. It seemed like the sky had cracked open. We all panicked, and Mr Tambu tried his best to calm all of the students, but some started crying, running around the classroom like chickens being chased by a fox. I sat at my desk, not moving, trying to work out what was happening.

The explosions grew louder as they got closer to the school. Through the window, I saw a massive cloud of smoke engulf everything in sight. I could hear children screaming outside my classroom. The screaming became louder and louder.

Through the smoke, I saw three old trucks laden with rebels pull up in the playground. They all jumped out and gathered next to the truck. None looked older than thirteen. The smallest looked about five. Every one of them looked different from the next. Their clothes looked like they hadn't been washed for a long time. Some faded, some ripped and others barely hanging on their bodies. They were all armed with either machetes or AK-47s. I knew the name of the gun because my father had told me as he read news articles about the rebels.

At the front stood a huge bear of a man. He was yelling at the group but I could not hear what he was saying. The crowd of rebels fanned out in four directions to storm the buildings. They were young enough to be students at our school. The bear man turned and looked towards me. I knew who he was. His name was Matete. He was a rebel commander. I couldn't see his eyes because he had sunglasses on, but his wild hair made my body quiver.

I had seen enough and ducked down, hiding under my desk. I had already wet my pants. Mr Tambu was shouting at us, telling everyone to run and never look back. I didn't run. Mr Tambu pulled me up and tried to lift me out the window. We could see the rebels assembling children into groups in the playground. Some, about my age, were being loaded onto the truck. I saw a rebel raise a machete to kill a young schoolboy. I realised later he was just too young to fight, so wasn't worth taking.

Seeing what was happening outside, Mr Tambu snatched me back from the ledge and shoved me into a nearby cupboard. As he shut the door I heard yelling outside, then another explosion. A grenade had been thrown into the room. The sound of that explosion almost left me deaf, but I could still hear fuzzy screams outside the room. Inside, there were no human sounds. I am not sure how long I lay there but eventually I opened the door and looked out. All the desks were overturned and

Mr Tambu was lying dead under some of them. So were other classmates of mine. I didn't know what to do, but I started to edge my way to the door.

Out the window I could see the trucks were gone and dead bodies were littered all around the playground. I couldn't see any rebels. Then I heard footsteps coming towards my classroom. I was going to hide back in the cupboard but I slipped on something wet and fell. The noise I made was loud and the footsteps stopped and then started again, faster, heavier. They were getting closer. Terrified, I knew death was imminent. Someone pushed at the door, which was half-hanging off its hinges, and my eyes widened with fear.

'Isa!' a voice shouted. 'It's me, it's me, Moïse.'

I started to shake. I couldn't believe my eyes, but as I felt my brother's hands reach under me and pick me up from beside the body of my dead teacher, I knew he was real.

Moïse put me on his back and started to run for home. Teachers were running in all directions ahead of us as we made our way through the schoolyard, past small bodies in blue-and-white uniforms laid on the ground like dead rabbits. Moïse jumped over a pile of corpses to avoid the river of blood that seemed to be flowing across the hard-baked earth. He only let go of me to wipe his face once.

The streets were burning. Smoke shadows hung over the city like the sky had lowered itself on a cloudy day. It felt like summer and winter at the same time. I inhaled the scent of roasting meat but it did not make me feel hungry. It made me feel sick. Moïse weaved and hid as we made our way along the streets. We hid behind a wall and watched as some of my friends were led away by a rebel with a gun. They had to hold their hands on their heads. I didn't know where the boys were being taken, but I knew it was a place I didn't want to go. I also knew that the quickest legs cannot survive the fastest bullet.

As we got closer to home we saw more soldiers. They were pushing people into a big house and we watched as they then set the house on fire. The people inside screamed for their lives, but the rebels were outside with guns at the ready to shoot anyone who tried to get away. Fire or bullet. It was no choice.

My brother and I ran from our spot and into the forest. Moïse half-carried, half-dragged me as we cut through the long grass to the path that led home.

As we approached the Ruzizi River, we heard the voices of angry boys from the opposite bank. They were getting closer and closer to us. They were rebels and we knew they would be armed.

Moïse turned around quickly and rushed to the river. He urged me to dive under the water and not to go to the shore. He pulled a couple of hollow reeds from the riverbed and gave one to me. He showed me how to breathe through it, with just the tip above water. We made our way underwater to the shelter of the mangroves on the other side as the rebels crossed the river and disappeared. Once the angry voices faded, we climbed out of the river and started running towards our house. Gunshots rang out in the distance. As we got closer to our house we could hear people screaming and crying. At the end of our street, we saw our neighbours running from every corner. Then, everything stopped. No one was running. It was suddenly quiet.

As quickly as the silence had come, bullets started to fly and people scattered. My body flinched every time a gun fired. Our LandCruiser was parked in our driveway, and from inside our house came the sound of a woman wailing. Her voice was loud and then all of a sudden, quiet. The quiet was louder than the screaming. The world stopped.

No man was shouting; not a single woman was screaming. The sun had fallen from the sky.

My brother signalled for me not to move or make a sound as he crept to look around the corner where we were hiding. I could see everything clearly from here.

Just as we were about to rush across into our home, a military truck full of rebel soldiers tore around the corner and screeched to a stop behind our LandCruiser.

The driver was the same man from the school. He got out as soldiers jumped off the back of the truck, shouting and yelling in different dialects as they stormed the house. Our house. They kicked the door open and disappeared inside. Some boys started smashing our car window with the butt of their AK-47s. Two more soldiers stood guard, machine guns at the ready. I didn't know what to do when the screams started up from inside the house. Men shouted. Glass broke. Furniture smashed.

Soon after, my father was marched out of the house at gunpoint. He was bloodied and bruising. We watched as soldiers beat him around the head and body with their weapons. My father seemed to be pleading with his captors but we couldn't hear what he said. But we could hear screams inside our house. They grew more bloodcurdling.

Moïse tried to shield me with his body to stop me seeing what was happening, but I couldn't look away.

When I saw my father being forced to his knees with an AK-47 aimed at his head I struggled to break free of Moïse's grip and cried out. Moïse clamped his hand over my mouth. Too late. Everyone looked towards the sound. One young soldier shouted an order and several others raced towards us. 'Run, Isa!' Moïse shouted. But the soldiers tackled us both to the ground.

They dragged us to where they had our father and forced Moïse and me to our knees. They tied our hands behind our backs. I kept my eyes down. I didn't want to see the faces of the rebel soldiers. They were wearing different coloured clothes. Some of the older rebels were holding guns, the majority carried machetes. They seemed like they hadn't washed for years. I could smell their sweat, mixed with something else, like the smell of lightning after the hottest day. I stared down at the soldiers' feet. Some of them had very long boots. The rest were wearing sandals.

I wanted to use the toilet but I couldn't. My hands were crying from the squeeze Moïse was giving them. I heard my mother screaming from inside the house and saw my father struggle to get free, but every time he moved, he was hit. A soldier slowly paced around my father. I looked over. The soldier was wearing long boots reaching up to his knees. The same type of boots my dad wore when he went farming with my mother. But the boots were too big for this soldier, bigger than his feet. He was holding an AK-47 pointed down with his finger on the trigger. He had a knife hanging on the side of his green shorts.

'Tell your commander to take me – it's me he wants!' my father shouted.

'Shut up! *Mjinga*!' The soldier hit my father in the head. He fell to the ground.

Just then, Matete walked out of our house. He was zipping up his trousers.

I heard my mother start screaming again, her voice getting louder and louder. Then, I heard a gunshot. My mother's screams stopped. Rita ran out of the house towards us. She was crying and her dress was torn, showing her breasts. Matete raised his weapon and shot her. For a moment it was as though her body was held up by strings, and then she fell, face first onto the path. Rita didn't move again.

Moïse screamed, low and guttural, like an animal in pain, and my father struggled to stand, lunging towards

Rita. The boy soldier kicked him again in the head. My father fell to the ground. 'Stay still, Moïse,' he shouted.

Matete walked over and placed his foot heavily on my father's back. I heard the air rush out his mouth. 'What am I going to do with you, imbecile!' Matete said.

My father gasped for air, winded as Matete stamped down on his back with his foot again. Matete called for someone to bring a shovel.

Moïse held tightly to my hand and I could feel him trembling. I pulled with all my strength to make sure he didn't rush at the leader. I knew the anger he would be feeling. I felt it myself. Anger and impotence.

Rita's body lay on the ground. Her blood had stained the earth black. The world was getting colder. There was no one to save us, nowhere to run for mercy. We were in a ditch without a hand to pull us out. Children with guns and machetes were in charge.

'Sometimes we cut people up before we kill them, sometimes we just shoot them. Stand up! All of you!' the child soldier yelled.

We were forced to walk over to the side of the road, and after they untied our hands they made us take turns digging a hole. We just kept digging, making it bigger and bigger. I watched as my father pushed the shovel into the dirt and turned out the soil onto a growing pile. His face was contorted, from pain and grief. He didn't speak a word as he dug. Moïse kept looking around, trying to find an answer that wasn't there. Finally, after we had all taken a turn to dig three times, we were ordered to stop. A gun was placed at my head as Matete told my father and Moïse to bring over the bodies of Rita and my mother. I closed my eyes tightly as they placed them into the hole. I heard my father and brother crying. The child soldier hit me across the face and told me to open my eyes. My father stood across from Moïse and me. His face was covered in blood, it had turned his white shirt mostly red. The soldiers laughed at him as he said to us, 'Stay strong. You're Alakis. Remember that!'

He had barely uttered the words when he was punched in the face and pushed into the hole on top of my mother and my sister. 'You don't talk, traitor!' Matete shouted.

But my father's voice was strong even from the bottom of a grave. 'Everyone has a chance to choose their fate, and if your fate is to destroy the lives of innocents, then sooner or later the hands and blood of those people you kill will consume you!'

'You think you're the Messiah,' retorted Matete. 'You're not the Messiah. *I* am the Messiah. *We* are the gods. We do whatever we want.' And Matete and two other soldiers swung their guns at my father and hit him over and over. My father was barely moving.

Moïse and I could not stop our cries. They pushed us onto our hands and knees. Matete's offsider thrust a shovel at Moïse.

'Do it!' he said.

With my father still alive in the ditch, my brother was forced to shovel dirt on top of him until we could not see him anymore.

It had become very quiet. All I could hear was the thud of dirt on top of my family.

My father was no longer.

My mother and my sister were dead.

Moïse and I were of an age to follow orders, the rebel leader said, and we must do as we were told. He said we would only live because we were the perfect weapon they needed. Our lives as we knew them were over. In one day the whole of our world had changed. And so had we.

ACT II

chapter 4

walking with nightmares

FROM THAT DAY, THE KID THAT I HAD BEEN WAS NO longer. I was to be taught how to kill and destroy. What my father and mother had built was to be demolished. And I had already realised that a hungry stomach is a much greater incentive than a full one.

I was on a new journey. With new faces. The same faces that destroyed my home and slaughtered my family. Somehow I had to learn to kill, but not kill them. There was danger there. My brother was now my only kin, and I knew that they should be afraid of him.

It seemed to me we had been walking for days, but we didn't ever reach our destination. I wasn't wearing long boots like most of the others, and my feet were scratched and swollen in flimsy sandals. The soldier in front and those at the rear and the side of us kept shouting at Moïse and me to walk faster. Every mountain we climbed seemed higher and every forest we passed through seemed denser than the last. There were other children the same age as me. Some were younger. Those who couldn't keep up the pace were killed and dumped by the roadside. Matete, the leader, shot a boy who walked beside me because he wouldn't stop crying. We carried any sustenance we could find, but we couldn't let that slow us down, or else we would be left behind for good. We had to keep up, sun past point midpoint. Words went through my brain as madness threatened.

I am walking down the track.
1400 hours.
Angry birds singing uncontrollably.
I can't get weak.
We're stepping on …
… sweet sound of fireworks.
Mud gets thicker, like we've been drinking liquor.
Clouds flicker.

The sun seemed to have taken refuge, covered by the rocky mountains that loomed above our heads. We were all soaked by an evening rain. We were told to make a shelter. Matete shouted, 'Make some fire and train new soldiers.'

Within the huddled group, I recognised boys from my school. Some were from the circle that enclosed me as I boxed in the playground and Moïse cheered me on. It seemed a long time ago. Most of my school friends had been shot in that playground. I had seen them lying in the dirt. Anyone who'd been captured was in the same convoy as my brother and me. We had passed the point of no return, we had no choice and no voice.

Sun past point midpoint.

Matete's main offsider, the boy I watched hit my father, was named Kadogo. He gestured to me and Moïse and led us to the edge of a hill. He was only a bit older than I was and younger than Moïse. We were told to guard the hill. To keep an eye out for any danger.

As night came down, the smoke from burning tyres made my eyes water. It was hard to see. And I was cold. I couldn't feel my legs.

After three hours the cold bit hard, and despite the smoke I wished I was closer to the fires. Kadogo was mumbling to himself. 'What am I doing here? What's the point? You live every day trying to survive the next. Who am I? I am on a mission with two instructions: kill everyone under the age of eight and over fifteen, and take the women and valuables to Matete.' I must have been staring at him because he glared at me and started singing, with his AK-47 hugged to his chest and a knife at his side. '*Wengi wame kufa, wadogo bado wana tembeya*', which means, 'Many are dead, only a few still live'.

'What do they call you?' he asked. 'What's your name?'

I didn't answer.

'His name is Isa,' Moïse said.

'No, it isn't. It's Cyborg! And you're Rambo! You can leave now,' he said as he gestured to Moïse with his knife.

'If he stays, I stay,' Moïse replied.

Kadogo slipped his AK-47 from his shoulder and pointed it at Moïse. Moïse looked at me and then walked away. I watched him disappear into the night.

'How old are you, anyway? Why aren't you talking?' Kadogo asked me.

I didn't reply.

'I am better off alone! I would have a better conversation by myself. Do you like stories? I had a puppy. It was so annoying. I mean, it wouldn't talk to me. Every time I looked at it, it just kept quiet! So, I shot it. That gave her a lesson! POW! You know, we are just the same you and me. I will always be here if you ever need me. Don't ever trust anyone else except for me. I will teach you things. Show you things. You are just like me.'

My face twisted.

'Yes, you are! You are lucky. You know I could shoot you right now and no one would care? I am invincible. No bullets can kill me. Not even a bomb.

'You know, people don't give a damn about you!' he continued. '*I* like you. Matete made me kill my parents, but I did you a favour. I killed yours myself. I am your only friend now. You'll respect me. My mother was pregnant. Only one week until she was due – the baby's name was going to be Lisa. My father was strong, but I sliced him into pieces. Your father was a weakling. *Weak!* I killed him like I killed my puppy. You can thank me for killing them. Have you ever killed anyone? You see, people will never give you the respect you deserve. You have to take it! Then when you are in charge, you can do whatever you want.'

My body started to shake as I listened to the boy who had killed my father. I didn't think it was possible to still have tears, but I did.

'You'll do as I say or I'll cut your ears off, then your nose. You see this?' Kadogo had moved over close to me and held his knife against my cheek. 'Unless you're a soldier, this is your worst enemy.'

Terror ran through me like an electric shock. Moïse was gone. He'd just walked away and left me. My family were dead. I had no one.

'I will do whatever you want me to do!' I said, unsure where the words had come from.

'Say it louder,' Kadogo demanded.

'I WILL DO WHATEVER YOU WANT ME TO DO.'

'Say you'll be a soldier!'

'You'll be a soldier!'

'Not me, you fool!'

'I will be a soldier.'

'Good! Stand up! A son of a traitor is a traitor. If you don't follow my orders I will slice you. If you try to run away, I will cut your head off. You hear me?'

'Yes.'

'What?'

'YES!'

'Your parents were bad people. They didn't care about you. Your brother didn't care about you. *I* am your only family now.' He pushed me to the ground. 'You'll respect me!'

Suddenly he yelped in pain. His hand went to the back of his head as he fell to the ground, dropping his gun.

Moïse stepped out from behind a rock, ready to fire again with his slingshot. Before Kadogo could gather up his gun, Moïse was above him with his slingshot pointed right at his head.

⌐

I HAD LET go of the child I once was and got to know the person I was becoming. I knew now my predicament was almost inescapable. Moïse couldn't save me; he had to try to save himself.

Matete had heard Kadogo's cries and Moïse had received a flogging for what he had done. Matete hadn't used a whip, he used his boots. They'd hung Moïse upside down from a tree, and all the soldiers surrounded him with their chicottes, giving him twenty lashes each. He cried until his voice left his throat. His tears drowned with cries. He didn't have a rescuer. If I were to defend him, I would also get the beatings.

I was made to sit on a bench near the fire to watch. Matete stood beside me, one hand holding my brother's slingshot, the other wrapped around my neck. Afterwards, Moïse's blood flowed fast from the whip marks on his body.

'I want this to be a lesson to you and your brother. And all of you little traitors. Next time I'll cut his head off. Do you understand?' Matete's voice was steady and strong and I had no doubt he would do as he threatened.

He threw the slingshot in the fire and ordered Moïse to be left strung up for three hours. I watched him walk towards a small hut, taking a young girl by the hand and pushing her inside before he followed. As the other soldiers looked at Moïse, I quickly snatched the slingshot from the fire. It was blackened but not burnt.

Another day passed. Much longer than three hours later, Moïse was finally cut down. I wasn't allowed to go to him and instead was made to scrounge for firewood for the camp. We hadn't been forced to walk anywhere that day and those who weren't given chores were ordered to march back and forth, and then stand at attention for a long time. It felt like the longest day when dark finally fell and we were all squeezed into small square huts. There was hardly room to breathe. We all slept face up. Every time I closed my eyes, the same nightmare would play over and over in my mind. I would hear Rita crying, the thud of earth on my father's back and the sound of the chicottes breaking Moïse's skin. Sweat ran down my bare chest. All of a sudden, my eyes sprung open. Moïse's face was above me. He tapped his hand on my forehead.

'It's okay, it's okay, it's okay. I'm here, Isa.'

My face collapsed into tears. My brother spoke to me in whispers, trying to comfort me without waking anyone else.

'Don't worry, little brother. I'm here. I'll always be here for you.'

'You'll never leave me?'

'I promise.'

'And I'll never leave you. I promise,' I said to Moïse.

I reached under my shirt, which I had laid my head on, and brought out the slingshot. I passed it to him, but he shook his head gently.

'You can keep it. Don't let anyone see it,' Moïse said.

'We are the only family we've got now, Isa. We're the Alakis. Don't you ever forget it.' He held my head against his chest while he patted me softly until my eyes closed. No nightmares dared come, because Moïse was there.

chapter 5

the birth of the beast

THE NEXT MORNING, WE WERE AWAKENED BY COLD water splashing on all the sleeping boys. I opened my eyes with a start and saw Kadogo standing at the door holding a bucket.

He looked hard at Moïse and then turned out of the doorway and disappeared. The rush of bodies to stand and follow him meant the smaller boys were pushed back. There was no kindness in the camp.

Morning drills began immediately. We stood in two lines, and the school uniforms many of us were still wearing were dirty and had started to tatter. The experienced soldiers stood in one line and the rest of us in the other. Matete paced between the lines, inspecting all and looking into the eyes of every child.

'Remember this. If you disobey my orders, I will kill

you. If you steal from me, I will kill you. If you try to run away, I will find you and I will kill you.' We all knew that his words were true.

We would sing songs after that. Mostly Kadogo would lead the song and the rest of us followed. *'Ngolô na Ngolô sangane, tû tendele ebalô'*, which means, 'all the mountains unite, let's stand for our country'.

As days passed and the weeks went by, we were taught to adapt and make decisions in a split second. The weak and defiant were killed. If you were smart – and Moïse and I were smart – you hid your hate and did exactly what you were told.

I learned how to use an AK-47. We were grouped under the shade of a tall baobab, said to be the biggest tree in the Congo forests. AK-47 parts were laid down on the ground and mine were placed on top of my shirt. Kadogo showed me how to assemble the gun and clean it. Moïse was a couple of metres down the row being taught by another experienced soldier. He often looked over at me and every time he did, Kadogo stared back at him. Other boys from my school were spread around as well, trying to build a gun. Matete wandered around all of us watching and commenting. He stood over me, and as he stared down, my fingers stopped working properly. He crouched beside me and took the carrier spring of the gun, slid it inside and then explained how a bullet leaves a gun when the trigger is pulled. He told me about the importance of every part of the gun and the importance of the finger that pulls the trigger to kill a traitor. As he said those words he got up and walked over to Moïse.

Kadogo placed my hand on the guard of the gun. I hesitated. 'It's okay. It won't bite you, come on!' he said.

Kadogo showed me again what to do. How to slot the carrier spring in the gun. How to lock the top hand guard in place. Once it was in correctly, he pushed the gas tube retaining pin down. Then, he took the bolt carrier and attached the bolt on it before sliding it into the gun. He pushed the bolt carrier towards the rear sight block. He took the spring, slid it in a hole inside the bolt carrier and then slid the back end of the spring into the small notch at the rear of the gun. And then, finally, he placed the dust cover under the rear sight block and the spring lock at the back of the gun. Kadogo checked it all again before putting in the magazine. He released the safety lever and then pulled the charging handle. He gave me the gun and mimed for me to aim and shoot.

After the session, my brother and I, along with the other new recruits, went into the forest to train. Kadogo marched us in and we were told to shoot at a target on a tree. We trained for hours – sighting, aiming, shooting. In between, Kadogo made us march drills. We trained until dark and then were told to rest.

I went to sit down, but Moïse told me to stay on my feet. He started talking to me about boxing, getting me to jab-jab-duck. He started to spar with me and I followed him every time he threw a punch. Every time he took a step. Every time he ducked. I did the same. I watched and paid attention. It felt good to be doing something that belonged to our old life, something that he used to love.

After a few moments, Kadogo signalled us to stop. He gathered us together. One of the soldiers on watch had spotted some civilians approaching and Kadogo wanted us to ambush them.

I used to be a civilian.

There were three of them. An old woman with a young girl, who looked almost Rita's age. A boy walked beside them and he was much older, almost a man. They were carrying sacks of cassava flour and fish.

We were to let them walk past and surround them from behind so they would have no place to run or hide. I was scared and wanted to run. But I did not want to die. As they got close Kadogo strode up to them and demanded, 'Give us all your money.'

The woman did not shrink back as she said, 'We have no money. We're taking these to sell in Fizi.'

The boy and girl stood behind the woman, and I didn't know what Kadogo was going to do. He raised his gun and grabbed the arm of the girl. She dropped the fish she was carrying. The man-boy, her brother, went to grab her, and his bag of flour hit the ground and split open. Kadogo hit him in the face with his gun. The woman started to cry and held onto her son's arm, keeping him still. Kadogo took the girl into the bush. I heard her crying, and saw the pain etched into the faces of her mother and brother – they could do nothing to help her. In front of them stood a bunch of boys, but when a boy holds an AK-47 he is more threatening and powerful than any grown man. After, the girl stumbled out from the bush into the arms of her mother. Kadogo stepped out too. He was laughing.

'You're all lucky today. Go now and return to where you have come from.' The three ran away from us, back down the track.

'You have to be tough, Cyborg and Rambo. You're now one of us. Pick up their food.'

Moïses and I did what we were told and made our way back to the camp. We watched the sunset turn the blue sky blood red as we walked.

⌒

ANOTHER NIGHT SAW us again squeezed into the small hut with no room to turn around and the air heavy with the breath of so many boys. The next morning, it was Kadogo's same wake-up routine: cold water splashed onto our sleeping bodies. Then another day of marching, shooting practice and being taught songs of victory. More new boys had arrived and this time we lined up in three straight lines. All the new boys were taken into the bushes near the camp, Moïse and I among them. We were told we were to be baptised, but I didn't know what that meant. They said it would make us invincible, take away our fear and give us strength.

We were lined up, facing a small hut that housed the elders. Unlike the other huts, this one was round. In groups of three, we were taken inside. Moïse and I were in the same group, and as we entered the hut we saw that the interior walls were covered in animal skulls, bird wings and antelope skins. It was dark inside, with only a small stroke of light coming through from the roof and the coals of a fire that glowed orange. It smelled like cooked cassava leaves.

Two men in ceremonial garb motioned to Moïse to step forward. They helped him undress and then gave him a small stick to clench between his teeth as they hit his back with the blunt side of their machetes. He didn't utter a sound, although it obviously hurt. Another elderly man, a witch-doctor, stirred a small broom-like utensil in a pan of water and herbs boiling over the small fire in the middle of the room. He brushed it over Moïse's body, slicking him with the boiling water. Job done, the men indicated for Moïse to go. As he left, it was my turn. I hesitated but my brother gave me a reassuring glance.

'Take your clothes off,' the witch-doctor said to me while he stirred a pan between his feet.

I did as I was told. The old man then flicked the boiling water all over me. I flinched, trying to remain still. But the water was so hot, I couldn't help but move. The old man signalled for me to turn around, and then continued brushing over my back. He did this while he chanted words. It was like he was singing, but it wasn't any song I'd heard before.

The witch-doctor took a small stick from the boiling water, said his incantations over it and gave it to me. He gestured for me to chew it. And then he asked me to face the two men with the machetes. Just as they had done to my brother, they hit me with the blunt side of their machetes, still chanting words I did not understand. After they were done, they asked me to walk out of the hut without turning back around otherwise it would break their spell.

The stick was approximately twenty centimetres long, and as thick as my little finger. They called it *mchinga*, meaning 'the root'. The witch-doctor told us we had to carry it in battles. And before battle we must not rob, eat leftover food, take a shower or sleep with a woman.

The next morning was different. At dawn, we were not woken by water thrown on us, just a shout from Matete to get up and outside. His voice had the same slap as cold water on my skin. We were loaded into three stolen government trucks that had arrived sometime in the night. We were told we were heading further towards Kalemie. Matete's truck was leading the way with the more experienced soldiers. The rest of us were in the last truck.

We drove into the mountains and as we travelled higher the wind got colder. I had to be vigilant and remember the rules given to me by the elders because we were heading into battle. Not to rob, eat leftovers or sleep with a woman. But Kadogo told us there was something else we had to do: take all the women to Matete.

Matete loved women the same way he loved his precious metals. He wanted to possess them for their beauty and the adornment or pleasure they could bring him. That was all that mattered to him. He did not care about the girls, and if they cried too much or screamed too loudly he would hit them or kill them, depending on his mood. A few days before, between drills and standing guard, he had forced me to rape a girl as a sign of our brotherhood. I didn't know how to start or what to do but Matete shouted at me.

'Rip off her underwear and put it in. It's easy!'

It wasn't easy but I did what I was told because I knew the AK-47 was close. Defiance would be punished. I couldn't look into the girl's eyes; she reminded me of the women I had loved. Tears started to drop from her eyes as she stared into mine. I avoided hers and kept my own shut, hoping Matete would tire of watching and let me stop. I don't know what happened to that girl. I never saw her again.

The trucks rumbled on and, soon enough, we approached a small village. Our truck stopped and Kadogo signalled for us to get out and go ahead on foot. The other two trucks continued on while we surrounded the left side of the village. The sound of explosions and the sight of smoke told us the others were in place. I could hear Matete's voice crackling through Kadogo's walkie-talkie, shouting orders. Kadogo motioned for us to split. My gun was ready for any danger.

The village was almost abandoned, with just a few civilians left. Our soldiers ran in and out of the houses, looting, shooting at anything that moved. They set fire to the huts with grass roofs. They didn't care if there were people inside.

I ran towards a small house. The door was locked, so I kicked it open and was inside in a split second. The furniture was already half-burnt from a long-ago fire and there was a gaping hole in the roof. There was no sign of life.

I looked out a broken back window and saw two men in government army uniforms approaching, creeping through the bushes with their weapons aimed at the village. They wore the same uniform Zeze had worn whenever he visited my father. They were getting closer. We had been taught to kill anyone with a gun or any government figure, and without thinking, I fired at them. Others did the same. Both men went down in a barrage of shots. I froze as I stared at the bodies lying on the ground. Had I had killed these men? Men who could be fathers or uncles, husbands and definitely sons? It was like I had killed my father's friend.

Kadogo burst in behind me. Seeing the bodies on the ground in government uniforms, he wrapped his arms around me in a hug. 'You're just like me, Cyborg,' he said. I shrugged him off and made my way to the next house. I couldn't see Moïse anywhere, but I was doing my job as a soldier.

I ran to another small house a few blocks down. It was too silent. I checked all the rooms and found nothing. But then I heard something from one of the bedrooms I had already checked. Someone coughed. I went and found a small boy hiding under the bed. Terrified. His hands on his head.

'You're coming with me,' I said.

The boy started crying and shaking at the same time.

'What's your name?' I asked.

'Jacob,' the boy replied. He looked younger than me. Maybe he was eight or so. 'You're not Jacob. From now on, you're Delta Force. Come with me.'

He didn't argue. I led him to our main assembly point, past burning homes and dead bodies. Delta Force was still in despair. He just stared and continued walking.

He's a quick learner, I thought.

Two of the stolen government trucks were parked in the street and a number of our soldiers were gathered around them. I saw Moïse was there. Kadogo appeared with a small group of new soldiers. He was shouting at them when a wounded government soldier half-ran, half-dragged himself from around a hut towards the trucks. He fired a handgun towards us and hit the boy walking next to Kadogo. As we all moved to take cover, he fired until he had no bullets left. One of our veteran soldiers ran towards him with his machete raised. The screams of the government soldier turned my stomach but I forced myself to walk towards him to help my comrade. I was a soldier now. A whole group of us surrounded the dying man.

'Delta Force!' I shouted, giving him my machete. 'Kill him!' The boy looked at me in horror. His eyes started dripping rain. 'Never look your victim in the eyes before you kill them. Otherwise, they'll stay with you forever. Kill him, Delta Force, do it now!'

The young boy looked at me and took the machete, raising it high.

Job done, we all climbed into the government trucks and left. Standing in the back of the truck, now wearing the dead man's uniform and long boots, I looked back at the bodies scattered around the village. My schoolmate's small body, shot by the government soldier, was there too. We didn't have time to bury him properly, so we covered him in burnt timber and bricks from the smouldering houses. We wanted to keep him away from the crows that would come, but the others we left in the open.

He would soon turn to dust, if the dogs didn't get him first. Next to me, Moïse looked at me, his eyes taking in the oversized clothes I had on and the holes in the cloth stained with fresh blood. I was no different from the rest now. I was no longer an innocent child. My brother could see the birth of the beast.

chapter 6

the fallen

BACK AT CAMP, THE NIGHT ENDED WITH A CELEBRATION of the successful invasion of the village. A celebration of the number of people we had killed. In the eyes of the militia, no one was innocent. I had already been told over and over and over, 'You are either for us or against us.' I was told I was lucky because I was with them, I was part of them. But it wasn't luck, it was self-preservation. If I didn't do as I was told, if I didn't do what a soldier had to do, I knew I would end up in a ditch just like my mother, my father and my sister.

Some of the boys played the drums while we assembled the wounded soldiers. Some had died in the back of the truck during the drive back. We piled up the dead. I went into a house to find kerosene and then walked over and poured it on the heap. Kadogo passed me a lit torch of fire and I held it to the liquid. Blue flame leapt and caught. I watched as the fire spread, and the smell and smoke made me turn away. I couldn't watch. I felt Kadogo's eyes on me but I refused to catch his eye. I didn't want to read what was on his face. Moïse was nowhere I could see, so I went and sat by myself under a tree and tried not to think at all.

I was learning the ways of a soldier. The ways of a beast. Sometimes we buried the bodies, sometimes we burned them, but sometimes we just left them where they had fallen or stacked them one on top of the other. When I thought about it, all I saw was my schoolmate lying on the ground. The image was always in the back of my mind. I didn't want to be like him and I did not want to remember. But there's a valley beneath all the tallest mountains.

While the bodies burned, Matete was in a small shanty with four women. I saw three women dragged in but the fourth stood tall and shook off hands. She disappeared through the doorway behind the other three. I did not want to know what would happen under that roof.

A game of soccer started up. Kadogo joined in, and Moïse was suddenly there calling to me to play. The game was highly physical and competitive, especially between Kadogo and my brother. We were all running around, kicking and enjoying the game despite the heavy ball. Kadogo targeted Moïse when he could but Moïse was too fast, too good. He would get his revenge when Kadogo ran with the ball: he would chase him down and steal it with his magic feet. It was only when someone kicked the ball outside the boundary and I went to pick it up that I saw. The ball was sweating and turning red. It looked like a human head nested perfectly inside a plastic bag. I turned away and started to throw up. The cramps in my stomach wouldn't stop. People were shouting at me to throw the ball back and when I forced myself to look at it again, it wasn't a head. I don't know what it was and I didn't want to find out. My mind felt strange and everything was so loud.

Other soldiers were on the sideline of our makeshift soccer field drinking *malofu*, a traditional alcohol made from palm trees. After cutting down a palm tree, they would remove all the palm leaves and cut the end off, wrap it with the leaves, and then insert a small tube through the middle to allow the liquid to flow into a jar. Fresh *malofu* tastes like wine, but if it is extracted a couple of days later it is more potent, and can make you drunk in under thirty minutes. I sat and drank what was offered, hoping it would stop me thinking.

The roads were silent. No trucks, no cars, no motorbikes. No people on foot. It was too quiet. Lions were ruling the streets while sheep hid.

Before the soldiers had come to my school, a soccer game had been common ground where children bonded. But this soccer game was different. There was a frenetic energy from every player, and fights and angry words broke out often. The game ended with no one a winner.

As the darkness came down another fire was built, a fire that burned wood, not bodies. All the soldiers gathered around to get warm and sing victory songs, with beer and weapons held tightly. Some soldiers waved their guns in the air. Kadogo sat next to me with a beer in one hand and the other wrapped around my shoulder. My brother sat outside the circle. It was past midnight and I could barely keep my eyes open.

Suddenly, Matete was among us. His face looked manic and he waved a handgun towards us as he started collecting all of the day's pickings. Mobile phones, jewellery and money. He said loudly: 'Soldiers! Well done today. Our next target will be Baraka. That's where we'll have another victory. But today we celebrate, for our new soldiers have become men. You're my children, and I'm your father!'

We all stood and gathered around him. My blood felt frozen and I wanted to throw up again. My old life was gone forever and I had to learn to not care about the ugliness, the blood and the death. My legs lost their strength and my stomach was crumbling, but I couldn't show weakness. The slingshot was hidden beneath my shorts and Matete couldn't see it. It gave me comfort. Reminded me of better days. I did not think I would see good days again.

With the fire burning and the boys gathered around him, it seemed Matete was a god. Matete was in charge, and no one could surpass him. From the stolen belongings, he held up a camera. 'What's your name, boy?' he asked, pointing over my head.

'Delta Force, sir!'

Matete threw him the camera. 'I want you to take pictures and videos when we go to fight. The world needs to know who we are and what we're capable of.'

'Yes, sir!' Delta Force responded.

Days went on like this, and every now and then someone would be given a task to do, a task that they had to keep doing until they were killed, or until Matete decided they had not done it well, and then they would still be killed. We were not his children then. Our rankings depended on our experience. Every time a new soldier was recruited, Matete would assign them to a group of twelve. The leader of that group was called *De Section*, meaning, 'the one in charge of the section'. Matete was the High Priest of the dozen – that's why he called himself the Messiah. Most times the new recruits would belong to the section of the soldier who had brought them in.

Kadogo was the leader of our section and he made me second in charge. I would give orders to soldiers below my rank, including my brother, and even to those who were not in our section. Recruited soldiers would only be given an AK-47 after their baptism. They would have to work hard, or kill someone who had one, to get one.

Our march continued. We were heading to Baraka, passing through the mountains of Kiliba, and everywhere we went we left more and more children behind. Some died from starvation, and some were killed because they couldn't keep up or did not obey the rules.

Delta Force, the soldier I single-handedly trained, was now terrorising other less experienced soldiers with a shooting game. He would challenge someone as we practised assembling our AK-47s – whoever finished first was allowed the first shot at their opponent. Delta Force always won.

We may have been losing child soldiers every step of the way, but it didn't decrease our number because we were also collecting new children everywhere we went. We would train them and keep moving. Once they were more experienced, they would be given an AK-47. Before that, a machete. We only used the machetes when we captured hostages. Sometimes we used them on anyone who didn't listen to our orders. We didn't waste bullets.

We climbed many mountains, crossed many rivers and passed through many forests. One day I could smell fresh water. Kadogo told us that Kalemie was only two days away from where we were. He said we would see it from the top of the next mountain. We weren't told why we were going there, we just had to follow the leader. I was exhausted. My feet were aching and my body was craving rest but there was no way I could stop. I had to remember to always obey the rules if I wanted to stay alive. That's what the witch-doctor had told me. I shouldn't steal, things or time, otherwise it would be the end of me.

Sun past point midpoint.

The village looked familiar, even though I had never been there. One of our trucks had pulled up but it was empty. I could hear gunfire and we could see a few dead bodies in blue uniforms lying on the ground. They were government soldiers from the FARDC – *Forces Armées de la République Démocratique du Congo*. I could hear Matete's commands through Kadogo's walkie-talkie, urging us on. No retreat. It was doomsday. There were few civilians in the village; they had been evacuated long before we arrived because they had heard we were coming. Those who dared stay behind would die, or be captured. It was an easy choice to leave.

Our new battle went on till sunset. We had a lot of wounded because the FARDC wasn't letting us through. Kadogo told me they were more resilient than they had been in the past. They weren't retreating. A third of the village was under our control, but we didn't have enough water and had counted on claiming the whole village and moving on to water much quicker. As night fell, the two forces secured their ground and rested, ready to continue the battle in the morning.

Kadogo's section claimed a small three-bedroom mudbrick house with a galvanised iron roof to camp in. All the wounded soldiers were put in one room. Matete claimed the master bedroom and the rest of us were spread between the third room and the main living area. We had stacked our dead outside, and would bury them if we had time the next day. Another child soldier from my school had been shot in his side; as he was helped into the room with the other wounded I heard him say, 'Finish me,' as tears fell from his eyes. I could smell the fresh blood and it made my stomach turn. I did not want to watch him suffer. He was better off resting in peace than waking in pieces.

Kadogo was leaning on the wall in the corner of the room. He was watching me while playing with his gun. Moonlight shone through the window, making everything a bluish silver, like it was a dream. Moïse was propped next to me, sleeping. I could hear the wind outside, making the tin roof creak, and I knew my mind would not let me sleep. 'It is time to either use a gun or a knife,' Kadogo said, nodding towards the room. 'A gun is faster but the knife is silent.'

It was a creed we carried for our brothers and our brotherhood, and I knew that Kadogo was telling me to kill my school friend. I heard my father's voice at that moment: 'You are an Alaki, you are better than that.'

I wanted to believe my father, to prove I wasn't born for this purpose. I wasn't born to be here. My dreams were far better than this. But I did not want to die. I knew what lay ahead was much more dangerous for me.

I didn't move, and Kadogo did not speak again. As time passed, the moans and cries from the room that held the wounded decreased. Silence was taking over.

Silent night.

They were gone, to a place we would all reach one day. I wished I could have asked them to greet my father and my mother. To take with them a hug to my sister, and to pass on my love, to tell them how much I missed them. I held my tongue and closed my eyes.

It was getting colder. Millions of memories were running in my head, more than the stars in the night sky. Finally I slept, face up, gun on my chest and a knife in my back pocket.

The light stole into the room as the day began, and the sound of a launched rocket made us all sit up fast. It was the sound of the loudest thunder you could ever hear, but every explosion was deadly. That sound made me want to poop and run at the same time. I wished I could lie back down and dream my way through that day, but I had to get up and follow orders. I had to focus.

Matete was the first one up. He took a minute to honour the fallen from the day before and then he said, 'Follow my lead if you don't want to end up like them.'

The day wore on. We were climbing up from the bottom of the hill that surrounded the village. Below the hill, at the end of the village, was the great Lake Tanganyika. Matete was urging us on, saying we couldn't slow down.

This was no place for children, and yet here we all were. Many of us were crawling along the broken ground. The only command we could hear was from god himself. He was screaming, 'Kadogo, you go with your men to the hill on the left. Prepare the rocket. Remember to kill everybody over the age of fifteen and under the age of eight.' How could we ever forget? That order was a constant at every battle.

We came to a crossroad where Matete had instructed us to separate and follow a different trail. Delta Force and Moïse carried a cannon. Kadogo had a rocket and I carried ammunition supplies. Others followed with machetes and guns. I had my AK-47 ready, looking this way and that. We silently fanned out deep in the bushes. Kadogo's walkie-talkie crackled at low volume amid the sounds of distant gunfire, rockets and people screaming. The explosions were getting closer. Kadogo signalled to us, pointing to our destination – a small hill overlooking the village – which was close by. We got to the top and he started to assemble the cannon. Smoke rose from below and we heard a sound that put us on high alert. Kadogo put his finger to his lips for us to stay quiet as he disappeared to check what was there.

Guns at the ready, Moïse and I crept down the hill, slowly. We found a stream and looked across it from bushes away from the bank. We could clearly see the village on the other side of the stream, smoke rising from every building. People were running around like crazy, screaming.

We saw a streak of colour among the green and brown of the bush on the other side, and as we edged closer to the bank, we heard a baby's cry. We hurried towards the sound and watched as a young couple tried to escape across the narrow waterway with their baby and a pile of luggage. They didn't know we were there. I looked at Moïse, we were frozen to the spot.

Sun past point midpoint.
I am walking down the track.
1400 hours.
I'm creeping through green grass.
Angry birds singing uncontrollably.
One, two, three civilians in my sight!
My gun is loaded and ready for impact.

Bones quiver.

My body squats.

Salty flood spilling down my chest.

The sun bursts in the blue sky.

My heart rusts with dust!

Burning rocks fly above my head.

Lift fists!

Sharp blades.

Skin bleeds.

Falling crows.

Let their shadows cover the ground like black sand!

My heart crumbles with thunder.

They get closer, so careless! I am fearless!

I can't get weak.

Sun past point midpoint.

I am walking down the track.

1400 hours.

I didn't see him there!

Gun loaded.

Two rounds up my sleeve.

Knife in my back pocket.

Ropes for silent nights.

They can't see me but I have all of them in sight.

Don't breathe. Keep quiet.

I am here for a demolition.

In the front line for a revolution.

She is carrying a sleepless baby whose noises stop my
heartbeats.

I slow down the time with caution.

See everything in motion.

Load my momentum.

Attack with aggression.

Frozen blast.

Broken glass.

Breathe.

The couple continued on, oblivious, then finally the man looked up and saw us. Before he could make any noise, Kadogo emerged from the bushes a little way down from us and shot him dead. His body splashed into the stream and the water turned red around him. The young woman screamed, clutching her baby to her chest. Pleading.

Her screams penetrated my heart like thorns. My mind was frozen. I was no longer seeing this young couple and their baby, I was seeing my father, my mother and my sister. The same painting had been repainted before my eyes, except, this time, my actions were conspicuous. Kadogo yelled at Moïse and me, gesturing with his gun.

'Are you out of your mind? They're cockroaches. Finish them! Go on! Finish them off.' He turned. 'You, slut, on your knees, now!'

The woman, terrified, had reached the bank and sunk to her knees, still holding her baby. Kadogo rushed towards Moïse and pushed him. 'Do it!' he screamed.

He shoved Moïse towards the woman and moved his arm, forcing him to hold the gun to the woman's head. My brother looked at me, then pulled his gun away. Kadogo turned his gun towards Moïse. 'I said, do it!'

'And you,' he said to me, 'smash the brat's head in.'

Moïse was defiant, holding his gun down, not prepared to pull the trigger, until Kadogo swivelled his gun to face me. 'Do it or your brother dies,' he said.

I watched a darkness cross Moïse's face and a tear run down his cheek. He fired, and the woman crumpled to the ground, her baby falling from her arms. Kadogo shouted, telling me what to do to the child. 'Do it now,' he said.

I could hear Matete's voice on the walkie-talkie, instructing us to launch the cannon. I took a step towards the baby and felt a rush as Moïse suddenly crash-tackled Kadogo to the ground.

'Run, Isa!' he said. 'Run!' he shouted louder.

Without hesitation, I threw away my gun and ran, ducking past the bushes. As I moved, stumbling, I heard a gunshot from where I had left my brother. I suddenly stopped to look back, but could see nothing. I heard more gunshots screaming like a machine gun. Silent night! I ran and ran until I was far away and couldn't hear the gunfire anymore.

When I couldn't run any longer, I slowed to a walk. The rhythm of my feet hitting the earth started to feel like a drum beat. I could hear my heart beating fast, thumping in my ears. I walked on, the sun getting hotter, and I started to hear the cries of small children as they were taken from their loved ones. In their voices I heard the cries of my sister. The sound of the baby falling from her mother's arms. A bullet tearing into flesh. The dull thud of a falling body. I heard the cries of all the fathers hung above dry branches and dumped into trenches.

I heard the sound of trumpets coming from the village I once called home.

I heard gunshots fired at people I once loved.

I heard the songs of praise, songs of wisdom, songs of sorrow being sung by women of all ages.

I heard the sound of an avalanche crashing down snowy mountains.

I heard the sound of waterfalls rushing down moistened stones.

I heard the sound of comrades shouting as they came to take my family away.

I heard the screams of young girls, crying as five men took turns.

Enough is never enough, but if you just say enough, it might be enough for people to get enough of it.

So, I say I'm guilty.

Yes, I am guilty for all the children I have killed with my bare hands.

And I am leaving you with this message.

I am sorry, for not doing my part.

By the time night came I was walking like a dead man, but my thoughts gave me no rest. I did not want to sleep because the nightmares would come. I did not know where Moïse was. And that was the worst nightmare of all.

ACT III

chapter 7

the clocks tick slower

FOR A TIME, IT FELT LIKE THE WHOLE WORLD HAD BEEN dropped onto my shoulders. I was hardened through no choice of my own, turned from child to man by war. I was alone, and I knew my decision to run that day would affect me tomorrow and tomorrow and tomorrow.

The mysteries of me getting to Kenya are still unresolved in my mind. I remember being on the shores of Lake Tanganyika in the DRC and sneaking onto a boat that was about to leave. Sometimes I walked, sometimes I asked for a lift. Most people drove past me, scared of who I was. But those who saw the innocent thirteen-year-old boy I had once been felt the need to pull up by the roadside and wait for me to hop in the back.

I was in a land of no man. Just another starving kid on the streets of Nairobi, with my hands up begging for anything from anyone. I was no longer that soldier-child who commanded, or received commands. I was almost free, but at the same time I didn't think I would ever be. When I closed my eyes I saw the horrors I had been part of, when my eyes were open I saw that I was alone. Every situation has its mountain, and I was facing mine.

Where I was didn't matter as long as I was as far from Kadogo and Matete as I could be, and yet my brother's life was still stored somewhere close to my heart. At times I wanted to go back to the DRC to find him, to trace where he had run to, but I didn't know where to start. At other times the thought of going back was too horrifying to consider.

I was begging on the streets. I was stealing food, money, clothes and anything I could find that would help me survive. I could justify all of this because I would not hurt anyone. I would just steal things, not lives. Not anymore.

My new home was beneath an abandoned apartment complex in the middle of the busy streets of Nairobi. The two-storey building sat at the corner of a main road and a small sandy lane. Partially crumbling at the top, this broken place was where I found some peace. The entrance was on the east side of the building but the door would not lock. There were two broken windows on each side of it and a rusty staircase that led up to nowhere. Built with heavy cement bricks, the stairs were raw and weathered. It was here that I would come as night fell and sleep in the basement, which was dry and sheltered and as safe as it could be. No one else lived in the building.

Outside, the streets never slept. The constant noise was a steady hum once I bedded down in my shelter. I could still hear the motorcycles, cars and bajaj. A bajaj is a large tricycle with a roof on top and can carry up to three passengers plus the cyclist. There was a motorcycle and bajaj station on the west side of the building, where at least fifty motorcycles and bajaj packs waited for customers, only thinning in number in the early morning before the sun rose. Near the station was a hardware store, a restaurant, a gambling office and a big hall that was always holding wedding ceremonies. Directly across the road was a supermarket that sold everything from body lotions to shovels.

I would go to the nearby restaurant every night to collect leftovers. There was an old lady there who took pity on me, but they refused to give me anything during the day because there were always too many people. If the old lady wasn't there I didn't get anything at all.

When I first arrived in Nairobi, before I found the apartment building, I slept under a tree every night. The building was much safer. Once it was dark and the streets were quieter, I would lie on the cardboard I used as a bed and listen to the sounds of crickets and geckos in the middle of broken walls, listen to the mice and rats I shared my space with.

I would hear people shouting outside most nights as drunks wandered around, into and out of the supermarket. They would argue like small children. The man with the fastest talk wins. Sometimes I would watch them from the broken windows.

In bed I would listen to the scuttle of cockroaches and wish that I was back in my bed in Bukavu. As I drifted off to sleep I knew that the nightmares would come, and I would tell myself that cowards flee but men face their demons. That I was an Alaki and I was not a coward. But I could not see those eyes I once learned from. Would never see them again. I was in a new place, meeting new faces, trying to accept these changes.

The clock ticks slower when you are waiting for the dawn. However, tomorrow is always another day. Every night before I closed my eyes I would say a short prayer taught to me by my mother: 'God, I know today was rough, but only you know my tomorrow.'

I would wake to the rumble of busy morning traffic. Very different from the noise I had run away from. These noises were friendly. They spoke of peace and harmony and normal life. I would dress and try to wash with any water I could collect. I am sure I became dirtier each day but I tried to clean myself up enough so I did not look like the lost child I was.

Every day I would stand at the same roadside, asking those who passed by for money or food. The unkindness of humankind made me feel like I was barely living. Most people walked past, avoided looking at me. Sometimes they kicked me, sometimes they threw water at me, but that was the least of my worries.

Although it had never crossed my mind that one day I would be in a country where people would look down on me like I didn't matter, I pretended not to be affected. I had had a future once. It floated in the back of my mind, my old dream, my old plan that one day I would build the most precious and iconic bridge in the DRC. But I no longer dreamed about that; it was like that was a different person's life. Someone I met once who whispered their deepest thoughts to me before they died. That person had died the day the earth was shovelled onto my father's face.

Sometimes I no longer wished to see another day. Sunrises only brought unresolved problems, such as finding food and staying out of trouble. I didn't dare think of my mother and the times she used to cook *ugali* with roasted *ndûbó*, or the fresh fish from the lake. As the last-born, I had always eaten the freshest food. Now, I ate whatever the old lady from the restaurant gave me, and the only thing I knew was that it was not fresh.

God, protect me from the evildoers. In the name of Jesus Christ. Amen. That was my daily prayer as I woke, before I had to get up and try and find food. The hungrier I got the more desperate I would get and the more likely I was to go against the good name of Alaki. My father would not have been pleased that I would steal or fight to feed myself. I was not honourable. But I was surviving.

Slowly, slowly, the streets became a part of me. I was a new person again. How many versions of me could I become? But I had to survive. It was normal to be a loner now. Safer.

There was a place a little distance from my building and the street that ruled my day. A place of trees, further down towards the ocean. It was one of the quietest places in the city, and I would go there sometimes but not too often, because thoughts of Moïse and my family waited for me there. And silence meant I could hear my thoughts too loudly. There was a path that led to the quiet place of trees, a path between two busy streets that was hidden from view because of bushes and buildings.

'God, forgive me for my wrongdoings. I know you understand.' I would say this each day before I did what I had to do. After saying my prayer, I prepared my feet and my fists, in case I needed to fight. In case someone fought back.

I could hear sounds. They were the sounds of humans. It was hard to see who was approaching through the bushes. Above my head, birds chattered.

An elderly woman, carrying a gallon of water on her head, was stumbling along the narrow footpath. I waited, steadying myself for my ambush – a skill I learned in my most recent life. Then, I heard more voices. Two men. The woman started screaming. I stared through a bush and could clearly see everyone. The two men were holding knives.

I recognised the woman from the restaurant; the old lady who gave me food. I would not let her be robbed by a couple of thugs, so I ran towards her. The two men looked wild. Their size gave me confidence: they were young, maybe fifteen. Older than me, but they had not seen what I had seen. I ran hard, with a wild look of my own on my face, and they shouted aggressively to me in a language I didn't understand. A language from further east, maybe. One of the thugs was wearing a grey T-shirt with black shorts, the other was in a black hoodie and blue jeans. The hoodie boy was carrying a cooking knife, and I punched him in his stomach and he fell down to the ground. He lashed out with his knife and tried to stab me, but I ducked and then was quick enough to hit him with a blow to the head. As soon as his friend saw that, he started running away. He was fast on his feet.

Hoodie boy stumbled to his feet and then he ran too.

'Thank you very much,' the old lady said. 'Those boys have been terrorising these streets like there isn't any law enforcement.'

I didn't have any words to say. After all, I had planned to do what they had done – without a knife, but with the same intent. I turned away and ran, leaving the old lady to gather her jug and get herself home.

As I ran, my thoughts jumbled together and I felt the tears roll down my face. Who I was no longer mattered. Frozen raindrops fell down from heaven like sons of giants. I stood on my corner and watched the motorcycles and cars and bajajs, and the rain soaked me to my skin. Thunder split the sky without mercy and every heavenly cry burst into my ears like a round of ammunition being fired. The sun had taken refuge above the clouds. It was ashamed of the men who had brought holocaust and atrocity to the world. It was ashamed of me. I was ashamed of me, too.

chapter 8

another isa

MY LUCK HAD GONE AND MY MIND FELT BROKEN. I
somehow made my way back to the derelict building
and sat staring out the shattered windows. Another day,
another sun, another struggle. As the street quietened,
I lay on my cardboard bed, but sleep would not come. I
held my slingshot close, thinking of Moïse and the way he
used to coach me to box. Getting up, I took a position and
started to practise my moves. *Jab-jab-duck*. It was a way to
feel close to my brother. All I had now were my memories
and his slingshot. But, after a while, I realised my stomach
didn't eat punches. It rumbled from hunger; all I had eaten
in the past few days were three bananas and a packet of
peanuts I stole from the supermarket.

Hoping for some blessing to return to me, I decided to
go back to see the old lady for some leftovers. But it seemed

the day was not going to return my luck and would instead add to my enemies.

The old woman was kind, and still grateful, and gave me enough food to feast on for a day or two. I was starting to feel better until, as I walked back to my building, a couple of bajaj drivers decided I should share my meal. One had seen me walking out of the restaurant and followed me, while calling over his friends. They stood in front of me and demanded I hand over my rice and beans. I was about to get mugged for what was rightfully given to me, and I still had enough of my father in me to realise the joke – the mugger was about to be mugged. I tried to fight but I was outnumbered and they took my food, beat me to the ground and left me unconscious by the roadside.

I was awakened by shouting that seemed to come from a long way away. When I opened my eyes, the old lady from the restaurant was leaning over me. She was talking to me in a soothing voice, and once I focused I could make out her words. 'You can call me Auntie. What happened to you? You are soaked like a drowned rat.'

I didn't know how long I had been lying there. I'd lost all sense of time, but the puddles on the ground told us both it had been raining.

'You will come home with me,' she said, as she helped me stand. I was wobbly on my feet and was not going to argue.

Auntie lived in a brick house a number of streets back from the main road. We walked there slowly, her body keeping me steady and upright when I felt the urge to sink to the ground. She settled me in a small room that had a petrol lamp hanging in the corner and a narrow bed covered by a thin mat.

She gave me some water and a slice of bread, and then left me with instructions to rest. I slept and wanted to cry at being again in a house, with the sounds of a woman bustling about and the smell of cooking drifting in the air. I could almost pretend I was home.

After two days of Auntie's care, I woke to a new voice outside my small room.

'Where did you get this one from? He sounds like trouble,' the voice sounded like it belonged to a young woman.

'On the streets. Looked like a drowned rat!'

'Auntie, when are you going to learn? You're not getting any younger.'

'He's a good boy, I know it. And I will help who I want.'

I heard plates rattling but their conversation stopped. I stayed in my room until they both left the house.

I didn't meet the owner of the voice until the next day. Nyota was a gorgeous seventeen-year-old girl with long braids that ran to her waist. She was wearing a blue dashiki with African flowers printed all over it. To me she looked like an African princess. She was tall and had an impressive strength about her.

She asked me where I was from.

'My name is Isa, I am Congolese.' I already knew what she was about to ask me next, so I told her first. 'I don't know how I got here.'

She just nodded. It seemed like that was all she wanted to know, which surprised me. I thought strangers usually liked to ask a lot of questions whenever they met a new face. Most people are unlikely to tell strangers their dark secrets, and I was not about to disclose mine. From that moment Nyota seemed to accept me and I was asked to stay, to help Auntie at her restaurant as well as to help Nyota with other small things, such as sweeping every morning, fetching water with her and selling water on the streets. She would often carry a bucket of fresh water and a bottle of juice and we would sell cups of them to drivers passing by, as well as the drivers at the busy stand at the corner of the main street. As the days rolled by I spent more and more time with Nyota. We would talk about the drivers we sold drinks to and laugh about the way they would try to show off for her. I told her about Moïse and how my brother used to teach me how to box, about gathering firewood with my sister and how my father had been a very important man.

On a day that seemed just like any other, Nyota brought me a bucket and dropped it by my feet.

'Here, scrub the floor. Scrub properly.' She didn't say please.

'Okay,' I said hesitantly.

'What is it?'

'Uh? Are you talking to me?'

'I don't see anybody else here. I saw the way you were looking at me. Is that what you do to get a girl's attention?'

'I don't know what you're talking about!'

'You are stupid!' Nyota said.

'And you say stupid things,' I replied.

'I don't date boys!'

'What?'

'I saw the way you were looking at me!'

'I was looking at your ...'

'Boobs?'

'No! I was looking at your ...'

'Bum?'

'No, I was looking at your ... uh ... head!'

'Right, I've heard that one before.'

'It's true.'

'Exactly!'

She took the bucket and left. I heard her laughing.

At first, Nyota became the best friend I'd never had. But, as time passed, she became something much more. I told her I needed to try to find Moïse, that I had to know if he was alive. But to do that I had to go back to the DRC, and I didn't know if I could.

Nyota and Auntie didn't want me to go. They were scared of what would happen – that I would be risking my life for nothing – and told me it was much safer to stay where I was. But I had no future in Nairobi. The only good thing I had there was Auntie and Nyota, and I knew how quickly what was good could be taken from me.

Every night Auntie would tell us both stories about her early days. She had grown up on a farm near Kisumu but one day her father had left her mother for another woman. From then on, she and her mother had been on their own.

Auntie was a very intelligent woman, she had attended high school, but she couldn't go to university because her mother couldn't afford the fees. She had no choice but to start helping her mother with the farm. It was hard work but Auntie was always looking for a way to make their lives better, and when she grew older she started selling small merchandise from the village to the larger shops in Kisumu. She grew her business a little every month and was proud on the day she could open a shop. Her mother was even prouder. Things were good for a while, but then a gang of thugs started hanging around, wanting her to pay them for their protection. She told them to earn their own money and to stop terrorising hard-working people. She thought they were young and full of words not actions. She stared them in the eye as she defied them and hoped they could not see her body shaking. For two weeks she did not see them, so she thought that she had stared them down, but then one night her shop was set on fire and she lost everything. The next day as she stood, numb, and watched the embers flare, one of the thugs walked by. He walked close to her and laughed a low, ugly laugh. She knew then she had not stared them down. They had made their point.

Bad luck kept coming for Auntie and, not long after, her mother passed away, so she moved to Nairobi to get away from the bad luck. And away from those thugs. She started selling food from a mobile restaurant. At first, she would just go to a busy street in town, set up and start cooking and sell to hungry workers on their breaks.

Auntie worked hard, but she knew what it felt like to have nothing, so she would give all the leftovers to hungry people on the streets who could not afford to pay. She started going to the local church and through them she began helping orphan refugees to get their refugee status in Nairobi. That is how she met Nyota. She saved her money and opened her restaurant in a shop front. I never knew how Auntie did as much as she did. And then she helped me.

Many years had passed since Auntie arrived in Nairobi. She told me she had four children, but I didn't know whether they came from her body or if she just collected them, like Nyota and me. I never met her husband, if she had one, and her children never visited while I was there. Auntie said they were busy with their lives just like she was with hers. She was almost fifty then but looked much older. She was a very tough woman with great stories. She told

103

me that, like me, Nyota didn't have parents and had been living with her for a long time.

It was Auntie who told me I could have a better life, that I could go somewhere else and start afresh away from war, AK-47s and thugs. I told Auntie I wanted to build bridges, and she told me I could do that if I went far away. I didn't want to be far away, though. What if Moïse had got away from Kadogo? What if he was looking for me? Auntie told me I owed it to my family to live and to learn. She was a lot like my mother, and her words made sense. Auntie helped me register with the United Nations as a refugee. She told me they had helped a lot of young men and women just like me; people who didn't have a place to call home. I said I would do it, and she booked an appointment for me to go and tell my story so I could become an official refugee from the DRC.

First thing the next Monday morning, I was in a small office. With only two glass windows that remained closed, the office was stifling. I sat in front of a small man who wore eyeglasses, and another agent, a woman who had a kind face. They were both sweating as if they had just come out of a shower. Just looking at them made me feel hotter as they organised the papers in front of them. The sound of a wall clock, tick, tick, ticking the seconds, was loud in the room. As the clock ticked on, they both asked me random questions and wrote down my responses.

'You have to answer these questions truthfully. Understood?' the woman with the kind face said.

'Yes,' I responded.

I didn't know how hard it was going to be. I had to relive the horrors I had seen, dredge up the feelings of watching my family being murdered, of listening to that gunshot as I ran and left my brother to … what?

I had to claim a new name. A name that to so many meant I was somehow lesser. I became a refugee. Now the entire universe knew of my new identity. It was a name I would have to carry for the rest of my life. Would it define me before all else?

I just had to be honest with myself and tell these two strangers who I was, but it was for me to decide who I was becoming.

A refugee.

Yes, I am a refugee.

You can affront me, confront me, or abuse me, but I promise that never will I cast a stone at you before I accept the fact that I am who I am today because of the cruelty and also the kindness of others.

Yes, I'm a refugee.

Who am I?

I'm that child who lived under the sun, surrounded by tears and blood under the palm. Yes, I'm that child who walked for miles to find that clean water.

I'm that child who lived under the gun with tears streaming down into the tarn.

You can think that calling me a refugee is a slur, but I am a survivor, a winner.

You show me where I've been, where I am and you'll know who I will be.

A refugee.

That day was the start of a new beginning. I left that small room determined to make that better life Auntie talked about, the life my father wanted me to have. The life he'd been fighting for, even though he must have known the danger. Nyota constantly said to me that yesterday no longer matters. I didn't believe her, but that day I knew I had a choice to determine how tomorrow ends.

I know that battles never end. But no matter how big or small they are, we have the power to rise above them. Or die trying. Like my family did.

It is said the truth should set you free. That day the truth did exactly that.

Sun past point midpoint.

I talked for a long time in that small room. I stopped hearing the ticking clock and forgot where I was. I was told to remember everything I said to those agents. My safety depended on it. I left not realising everything was about to change again.

The next day, I went back to my routine. It was like the room had been a dream. I helped Auntie at her restaurant. Then, in the afternoon when the roads were busiest, Nyota and I sold food and drinks on the streets. Nairobi is hot and motorists would always be thirsty, stuck in traffic. We would approach them whenever they stopped their cars and sell them the water they were craving. Normally, as we walked together, Nyota and I would talk about everything and laugh at the way the motorcycle riders would swerve as they pretended not to be looking at her long legs. The day after I had been in that room we were both quieter than usual, each lost in our own mind. But having her there still felt good.

As the sun dropped lower in the sky, we went home to Auntie's, where she was waiting for us with a meal. It felt like going home. And yet that night I also felt the slight stab in my heart that it was not my mother I was going home to.

Auntie's food was good, but my mother's cooking had tasted much more delicious. We'd always eaten traditional food as I was growing up, I knew no different. But now I did. Sometimes Auntie would ask me what I used to eat and when I told her fish, she came home with a long skinny one, the size of three fingers. But it was not as tasty as the fish we used to catch in the lake. I never told Auntie that, or compared her cooking to my mother's. I was grateful that she took me in and treated me like her own son.

Working in the restaurant and selling small things on the streets with Nyota became my daily job. I earned a couple of shillings. Enough to buy a pair of shoes and new underwear when I needed them.

Two years went by, and Auntie looked after me. I was sixteen and still trying to find Moïse. Nyota helped. We would sell our wares and then take a break to visit another office in town. The Red Cross, UNHCR, they were all trying to help me. Kind people in small offices would tell us that they were still searching for him. The staff at the Red Cross office told me they were good at finding missing persons. They told me that they would be sure to let me know when they had a lead. But two years had gone by and there was still no lead.

Auntie would sometimes look at me and say, 'You're a strong boy. You're like my son.' It made me happy and sad at the same time when she said those words. Happy for what I had. Sad for what I'd lost. And all the while we both knew that one day I would have to make a choice to chase that better life.

chapter 9

too many goodbyes

'Isa, now that you're a refugee, you can apply for resettlement to go anywhere in the world!'

Nyota and I were walking home from fetching water and she had started talking about what I should do. She was like Auntie, wanting me to chase something better.

'I don't want to go anywhere. I want to go back to Congo to find my brother.'

'They will kill you if you go back. You can't. But we could go somewhere together.'

'I don't know, we can't leave Auntie.' I didn't want to lose what I had for something I didn't know. I would never tell them, but I was scared.

'Isa, Isa! Watch out!'

I looked back and saw that Nyota was about to hit my shoulder. I watched as she started to box at the air, the way she saw me do in the afternoons as I did what she called my 'training'. The fear niggling at my brain started to ease and I laughed. Her eyes narrowed like they do when someone is deciding to be angry. But then she smiled and said, 'My name is Isa and I can knock you out.'

'You see, you don't even know your own name,' I said.

She stopped and laughed. 'Are you actually good?'

'At what?'

'Boxing. Do you think you can knock me out in one minute?'

'Uh ... Nyota, don't be stupid.'

'Why do you like fighting?'

'Moïse told me to protect myself. He taught me everything I know.'

'Tell me what he told you.'

'I don't know about telling you, but I can show you.' I stepped towards her. 'Okay, first of all, bend your knees. Put your left hand here, a bit higher. Higher. And then your right hand here.'

'Then what?'

'Jab, jab, duck ...'

'What's that?'

I showed her. She tripped and almost fell down, but I caught her. It felt good to hold her close, and when I went to speak I couldn't find the words. We righted ourselves but my hands had trouble letting go of her.

'What?' she asked.

'You have a nice … head.'

We both laughed and walked on. But we walked closer so our bodies touched.

⟵

THREE WEEKS LATER, I applied for resettlement. Nyota and Auntie had talked almost non-stop about it for the three weeks before, and though Auntie looked sad after we talked, she told us both that I needed to do bigger things. Things she wished she could have done. I went back to that same small room and I was in there for two hours with three immigration officers. There was no person with a kind face this time. No one smiled. They pounded me with endless questions. And they all wrote my responses down on their papers in front of them.

'How do you say your name?'

'Eesah Alakey.'

'How old are you?'

'Seventeen.'

'Why do you want to leave Africa?'

'Because I cannot go back to my home.'

'Why is it that you cannot go back?'

'I will be killed!'

'Who would kill you if you go back?'

'Many people.'

'Do you have any family in the DRC?'

'I have a brother.'

'Have you ever been involved in any criminal activities? Have you ever committed any war crimes? Have you killed?'

Have you killed?

'I don't know.'

'Yes or no?'

I couldn't speak.

'HAVE YOU KILLED?'

I didn't know how to answer that question. My father used to say that people like Matete would face justice before God and the law. But wasn't I the same as him? Maybe I deserved that same judgement. Had I shamed my parents? Had I disgraced the Alaki name? I felt shame. But when the choice was to kill or die would God judge me the same way he judged Matete?

I told the officer that I did not know. A single tear rolled down my cheek and I stared into his eyes, hoping to see some understanding, some kindness. He looked away.

Five months later, on a Thursday, a UN officer called Auntie's house. They asked me to go back to the office to collect a letter. I went with Nyota the next morning and this time, the kind lady was there again. She was very happy to see us and told Nyota to wait while she took me into another small room. A different one. It was much cooler. It had a window that was open. We sat down and she started to talk. She told me she believed it was unsafe for me to go back to my country and that they had been working hard to find another place for me. She said they had finally found me a country I would call home. She handed me a sealed letter and explained that I was to go to another office at a different address to meet other people for a further assessment.

Nyota and I left the office. Nyota wanted to know what happened. She kept asking and I said nothing, just kept walking faster so she was practically running to catch up. She snatched the letter, and I didn't stop her from opening it.

She read aloud:

Dear Isa Alaki,

Congratulations, you have been accepted for resettlement in Australia.

You have been deemed to be a refugee, because it is unsafe for you to return to your homeland.

As part of the process, you are expected to undertake a medical examination and security checks in order for you to immigrate to your new country, Australia. These will be conducted at 10am, on 17 May 2005 at the UNHCR Headquarters, Lynwood Court, Westlands, Nairobi.

Your travelling dates to Australia will be confirmed three weeks after the examinations.

'This is great news! Do you know what this means, Isa? Isa. ISA!'

'Leave me alone.'

'What's wrong with you?'

'LEAVE ME ALONE!'

'What's going on in your head? You've just been accepted to Australia; you should be happy.'

115

The realisation of what the lady had told me, what the letter meant, hit hard.

'I have to find Moïse!'

'You'll have a much better chance of finding him from there, and I will help you look for him from here!'

'I don't want to leave you and Auntie. I don't want to travel further away from Moïse. Do you even know where Australia is, Nyota?'

'Yes! It's in ... it's in, uh ... I don't know okay, but it sounds like a safer place. Once you're there, you can bring him. You know I've been waiting for this chance for so long, but you're lucky. You should be thankful, Isa. Not many people get the opportunity to go after being here for just a few years.'

'But I know nobody there.'

'You will still be talking to me. And I don't want you talking to white girls there!'

'Why not?' Nyota's face looked angry, and before she could say anything else I said, 'Fine, I will only talk to ... black girls ...'

'Good, because there are no black people in Australia anywhere!'

'What?'

'I read it,' she said as she skipped away from me with her hands in her pockets and a big smile on her face. She loved to trick me.

'Where?'

'I'm not telling you! What are you going to get me when you get there?' she said as she approached me again, standing only a few centimetres away from my face.

'Something special.'

'Like?'

'A pair of shoes?'

She laughed softly. 'That's not special, Isa.'

All of the sudden her mood changed and she got serious. We walked back to Auntie's place without saying a word. You could cut the air with a knife. As we turned into our street I was about to ask her what was wrong, but Nyota's words were first.

'I will miss you.'

She forced a smile, but her face was filled with sadness.

'I will miss you too, Nyota.'

↩

NYOTA PRACTICALLY SHOUTED the news to Auntie as we walked in the door. Auntie was very excited for me and said she had to prepare a meal for us, to celebrate. She cooked *ugali* and rice with *sato*, a delicious fish from the ocean. She also cooked a soup of goat meat. We ate as a celebration, but I didn't want to look at Auntie's face, or at Nyota. They looked at me with joy and pity at the same time. I know they didn't want me to leave, but they both wanted me to find a better life. The thought of leaving them made the food stick in my throat. It was hard to feel excitement. I felt I was losing something precious again. That night the tears came and I couldn't sleep. I thought I heard Nyota crying, but I decided it was just the wind.

The following days were busy. Nyota and I still worked, but I went for my medical checks. When I arrived I saw ten or so families there, all part of the same program and planning to leave for Australia at the same time as me. We were taken to a large room and shown a film about all the things we could expect to see in Australia. They showed us all the major cities and then talked about the unique animals. It looked like a beautiful place.

I went home that night and told Nyota and Auntie what I learned about Australia. They listened, but Nyota seemed angry. As it got closer to my leaving date we both had moments when we would yell at each other and Auntie would have to step in. It was like the closer it got to saying goodbye, the easier it seemed if we were angry with each other. But even that did not make it easy. On my last night, Nyota sat on the side of the road with her head on my shoulder. She cried and I told her that we would always be family. I promised her we would see each other again soon. I don't know whether either of us believed what I was saying, but we stopped being angry.

The morning I left tore at my heart. I hugged them both hard as tears dropped down Nyota's face. Auntie held my hand and said, 'Good luck. You're a strong boy and I know you'll be fine.' She turned and walked back to her house but I saw the tears in her eyes. I didn't think I could leave another family behind, but the driver of the ute who was taking me to the airport signalled that we had to go. I stared back as Nyota waved, growing smaller and smaller through the back window. She was still waving as we turned a corner, and then she was gone.

chapter 10

a new world

WE DROVE FOR ALMOST AN HOUR BEFORE WE GOT TO THE airport. Every time the ute slowed I wanted to jump out and run back to Nyota and Auntie. But something stopped me. I heard my father's voice in my head saying, 'You are an Alaki, you can do something bigger than selling water on the street.' As the ute pulled up at the airport I told myself I had to be strong, I had to be like my father and mother who had travelled from their places of birth to start the Bembe tribe somewhere new. That was what I was going to do. I would be brave like they had been.

The airport was busy, people were rushing around and the sound was a steady buzz until a plane took off – then there was a roar that made everything else sound like a whisper. It was my first time on a plane. My legs trembled as I walked up some stairs into a big container with wings.

Many small chairs were stuck together, arranged as in a church. I sat down and was told to buckle my seat belt. We may have all been sitting tightly together like we did in church, but no one was singing and no preacher was before us. I had to look over the heads in front of me to see where the seats ended. Everyone concentrated on what was in front of them: a small screen, a bit bigger than my palm. I stared out the window as we took off and watched everything below get smaller and smaller. Somewhere down there was Nyota and Auntie, and as we crossed over water and mountains I wondered if Moïse was looking up at the plane I was in. I liked the feeling of travelling somewhere else, and with so many people around me doing the same thing I started to lose some of my fear.

Hours went by and it was like the world had shrunk down just to us. But then the man next to me started snoring and all I could hear was his rasping breath and it made me want to get where we were going as fast as we could.

Sometimes the plane would shake. When that happened I was scared and thought I was going to die. Every now and then a woman with a brightly coloured scarf would offer some food that didn't make sense to me. The food looked strange. She also brought fruit, but I didn't know what it was, so I never ate it. I wanted to get to where we were going so I could eat *ugali*. This food wasn't enough to make me full. I went to the toilet but couldn't see the hole, and I couldn't ask anyone anything because my English wasn't very good. The white people couldn't understand me and I couldn't understand them. I had to hold on, but when we landed in a place called Bangkok a man saw me in the bathroom and he explained what to do. I felt so much better without my bladder full.

After a lot of sitting down in this container with wings, I finally landed in Brisbane. As I walked out into the airport arrivals hall I saw a small woman whose body seemed like that of a child, but whose face looked as wise and old as a hundred-year-old woman. She was holding a small cardboard sign with my name on it.

Isa Alaki.

She was standing with an African man. Nyota had said there were no Africans in Australia, so how come I was being welcomed by one? I was disappointed. I thought I was going to be the only black person in the country, which would make me special, but someone had made it before me.

I started walking towards the couple.

'You must be Isa?' the African man asked in Swahili as I approached.

'Yes, I am.'

'I'm your case worker,' the lady said. 'My name is Ms Li and this is my interpreter, Mr Amisi Dieudonne. We are from the Multicultural Development Association. How was your flight?'

Mr Amisi translated Ms Li's words for me but I didn't want to tell them about how I felt when the container shook, so I just smiled. Mr Amisi took my small bag instead, and we headed for the door.

'Amisi is Congolese as well. He will assist you if you need anything. You'll be able to contact him because he speaks Swahili,' Ms Li said.

I'd known right away that Mr Amisi was Congolese because he had a Congolese name. Amisi means 'Gift of God' in Swahili and his last name, Dieudonne, was a French name: *Dieu*, meaning 'God', and *donne*, meaning 'give'.

As we got outside, I was welcomed by a strong heat that almost fried my skin. It felt like I was putting my face in an oven. I was also surprised to see the sky, and that the sun was even bigger than the sun we had in Africa. Walking towards the car park, I looked across and saw a forest. I was suspicious about what I was seeing; I thought maybe I was still in Africa. Regardless of seeing the sun, trees and the sky, I knew that my house was going to be one of those tall buildings like the ones they had in Nairobi.

We started driving, and soon I could see the city: high-rise buildings, whose windows shone like little suns at the edge of a river. I was very excited to find my new home, but I was surprised when we started driving away from the tall buildings. For the next thirty minutes we drove, passing houses and small shops with large fields of green, and everywhere there were trees. Ms Li finally stopped at what looked like an abandoned house. The grass out the front was longer than the other houses on the street and it was mostly brown, whereas the two houses to the right had green grass out the front. It looked lonely.

'You're home,' she said.

I looked at the house; it was very different from how I had imagined it would be. I asked Mr Amisi, 'Why is the house on stilts? What if it falls down when we get inside?'

'Most houses in Queensland are on stilts,' he responded in Swahili. 'But don't worry, there have been many people who have lived here for a long time and never did the house collapse. You'll be fine.'

We went inside and Ms Li opened up the windows. She showed me through the house and pointed out the bathroom and three bedrooms, showing me the one I would use. There was a lounge and a table and chairs, and Ms Li told me there were two other people living in the house – one was away at an intensive language course and the other was on shift work, so I would only see them fleetingly and should try to keep quiet in case they were sleeping. She told me that I would stay here for a few days and then I would move into a unit on my own. She suggested we sit at the table so she could go through all the information she thought I would need. Mr Amisi went into the kitchen, a small room off the main one, to make us coffee.

My eyes were scratchy with the need to sleep but I didn't want to say that to Ms Li as she gathered pieces of paper to show me. She placed a pad and paper on the table and then nodded before she said, 'As I told you earlier, I will be your case worker until you are able to find things on your own. I will take you to a doctor, show you where the shops are and help you buy your food. In case of any emergency, you can call this number.' She handed me a square card and showed me where the phone was on the wall in the kitchen. Mr Amisi had returned with our drinks and relayed what Ms Li was telling me.

'Do you understand?'

'Yes,' I replied.

'What languages do you understand?' Ms Li asked.

'Swahili and a little bit of English and French.'

'Would you say your level of English is poor, intermediate or advanced?'

'In the middle.'

'Can you read and write?'

'Yes.'

'What is your faith?'

'Christian.'

'Do you sing?'

'No!' I laughed at that one.

'Do you play sport?'

'Yes.'

'What's your favourite sport?'

'Fighting.'

Ms Li looked up from her paper and said, 'You mean boxing? We'll help you find a place where you can train, and also enrol you into language classes so you can improve your English.'

Ms Li and Mr Amisi stayed for a long time. Mr Amisi showed me the bathroom to make sure I knew how the toilet worked and then in the kitchen he explained the oven and the microwave, warning me not to put any metal inside it. I didn't know exactly what he meant but I told myself I would work it out. He showed me the hot and cold tap and explained that in the shower the hot water came out fast, so I should turn the cold on first. They had arranged for food to be delivered, and after we ate a meal together Ms Li showed me where things went in the kitchen. I was used to chores at Auntie's, so I knew what to do, and I knew how to use every appliance they were showing me. I had used them back in Nairobi.

It felt like the day had lasted a week, and when they left, all I wanted to do was lie down and sleep. The house made noises I had never heard before and there was no bustling traffic outside, just the sound of birds calling. But it was not the birdsong I was used to. I could hear what must have been crickets, but they sounded angry. I tried to sleep but couldn't, so I turned the light on and listened for someone coming home. I pulled Moïse's slingshot from my bag and put it under my pillow. It was one of the only things that could bring me comfort, but I felt very alone and wondered what Auntie and Nyota were doing right then.

As I started to doze, I suddenly jolted upright, sure somebody was outside my room waiting to shoot me. I got up and opened the door slowly, straining my ears, thinking I could hear Matete's voice coming through on the walkie-talkie. But there was nothing but the sound of a dripping tap. I told myself that I was in a different country and Matete would not find me here. But that meant Moïse couldn't find me either and I felt my blood start to slow and my heart start to hurt as I realised I was completely alone.

Somehow I slept, and when I woke the house was hot and the sun was high in the sky. I got up and drank water from the tap and wondered how I could make this strange new place my home. Everything felt upside down.

Ms Li and Mr Amisi came the next day to see how I was settling in. They waited while I showered and then took me to an office building. I knew about offices, so I felt a little calmer, but it turned out to be another place for lots of questions to be asked. We stayed in a line for almost an hour before we could see the lady behind the desk, who never stopped asking me questions. She gave me a card with 'Centrelink' at the top. After I was done, we went to the doctor, where I was asked more questions. After that, they took me to a bank and set up an account for me. They told me that I would have money in there to get me started, and then Ms Li and Mr Amisi took me to a machine that throws up money.

'This is an ATM,' Ms Li said. 'You put your card inside, key in your pin number and the amount of money you need, and the machine gives it to you.'

Ms Li told the machine to spit out fifty dollars, and it did. She gave it to me and said I should buy anything I needed.

I told Mr Amisi that I thought everyone in Australia must be rich if there's a machine that spits out as much money as you want. He laughed and explained that the machine would only give you money that you earned, and that for a while I would get an amount of money from Centrelink but that once I spent it I wouldn't get more for two weeks, so I had to make it last. And I would have to get a job. It all seemed so strange and I wasn't sure what I could do but I told him I would work hard.

After more appointments in more offices, I was taken back to the house. I asked if I could call Nyota and Auntie at the restaurant to let them know I had arrived safely. I couldn't wait to tell Nyota that I'd found Africans in Australia and also that the sky and trees existed here, just like in Africa. Ms Li told me I could but to make sure I didn't talk longer than five minutes.

I listened to the phone connecting and wanted to cry when I heard Auntie's voice. I told her I was okay and that once I got a job I would send them money to help out. I didn't tell them about the machine that spits out money because I knew they would want me to ask the machine for money for them. I told her that most houses in Australia lived in the air. She laughed hard and said she wanted to see.

Then Nyota got on the phone. I told her I missed her and that I hoped she would come to Australia. I asked her to keep checking at the Red Cross and UNHCR to see if there was word on Moïse and she promised she would. I didn't stay on the phone long but I felt strange to be so far away and yet to hear their voices so clearly. Stranger still to say goodbye once more.

That night I couldn't sleep again. The sounds of the house were very different to the sounds I was used to. I lay in bed and listened to the whoosh of the wind under the floor and imagined the house rising and falling on every gust. When I closed my eyes I saw Nyota's face. I wished I was with her. I felt lonelier than when I'd first arrived in Nairobi. But back then my mind was broken and I couldn't feel. Now I felt everything, and all the memories of the past few years tumbled together in a mangle of cries, screams, blood and sorrow that brought nightmares when I eventually slept and sadness when I woke. And I thought of Moïse. Was he alive? Did he escape? Would I see my brother again? I reached under my pillow for the reassuring touch of his slingshot.

The next morning, I walked down my street to a nearby shop to buy bread. Cars drove past me but nobody else was around. After ten minutes of walking, I got to the shop but I didn't know what to tell the man behind the counter. He was the whitest man I had ever seen but his nose was red. He looked at me and smiled. I just smiled back and walked in. Without knowing which aisle to go to I walked up and down the whole shop until I got to a section where I saw bread. Well, I thought it was bread – but it was what I later discovered was the cake section. It looked so different but I didn't know what to say to the man to ask him where the bread was. I took the cake and went to the register, gave the man the fifty dollars and walked out. Those first days were hard. But slowly I started to understand what to do, what to buy, how to pay and where to go.

I moved from that house to a unit closer to the city, and a few weeks later, Ms Li took me to Milpera, a special school for people for whom English is their second language. She rode on the train with me to show me which train I should take and which station I should stop at. We were on it for more than half an hour before we got off to take another train to the school. We stopped at Roma Street train station. That's where there were many more trains. Here there were lots of people walking; many people in a hurry.

I started travelling to the school every day at the same time. The people around me never smiled or said hello. When a group of people walked past me in a hurry, I always thought maybe they were running from something, so I would stop and look back to see what they were running away from.

It was a strange time for me. On my first day at Milpera I met many Africans. I tried to greet them in Swahili, but they didn't seem to understand what I was saying. They looked at me like I wasn't there, like they couldn't hear me. I didn't belong. There were many Asian people at the school too and they all spoke different languages.

The first morning, the teacher walked into the classroom and introduced herself. Then she asked me to introduce myself in front of the other students. I didn't know what to say. Australian English is very complex, so my answers to questions when Mr Amisi wasn't around consisted only of yes or no. I stood, not saying a word.

'Isa, where are you from?'

I answered, 'Yes.' My responses to questions would depend on how the question was asked. If the person sounded aggressive, then I would answer, 'No.' I went to school every day and tried hard, but I was listening to a teacher I could not understand. After that first day, I didn't want to return there. I didn't want to stay in the corner alone and never know what was happening. None of it was helping me find my brother. After that first week I didn't want to talk to anybody, and nobody wanted to talk to me.

Ms Li had told me to call if I needed her, but she was a busy woman looking after many refugees. Mr Amisi told me to call him, too, but I didn't like talking on the phone.

When I wasn't at school I would walk around the city, and people would look away when I looked them in the eye. They seemed scared. One day I went to the machine that spits money and took some cash out and went to the shops to buy a small audiocassette radio with earphones. I also bought a few random cassettes and I listened to the music every time I was on the train home or on my way to school.

Sometimes I would get off at Central station to buy ice-cream from McDonald's. It looked like *éfunde* placed on top of a triangular cardboard. *Éfunde* is a type of food – soft cassava – that my mother used to cook in the DRC. She would leave piled cassava in water for a week or so, and once it was soft, she would remove it from the water to give us *éfunde*. She would do that because some cassavas are bitter and after soaking, all the bitterness leaves. She would then dry the wet cassava in the sun or with smoke under the fire in the kitchen. Once it was dry, she would pile it up again and smash the dry cassava with a rounded rolling pin to make semolina.

My mother would only make *éfunde* on special occasions; most of the time my father would buy it from the market. Eating that McDonald's ice-cream was a way for me to hold onto a good memory of my mother. Something other than her screams that would echo in my head at night.

After three months I didn't feel like I was learning

enough. I wanted to study and get my engineering degree but I still couldn't understand a lot of what was said. I asked Ms Li if she could help me find a job. I wanted to earn money to help me find my brother and also to help Auntie and Nyota. Ms Li registered me with a work agency, and I would go there every day after school to ask about a job. No one wanted to take me because I didn't have any experience, and my English wasn't any good. Every day I would tell them the same thing: I was ready to do anything as long as I was getting paid.

I called Auntie and Nyota a few times and Nyota had called me once, but it had been weeks since we had spoken and I had nobody else to talk to. I would come back every night to my small one-bedroom apartment and wait until the sun came up to do it all over again. It got quieter at night in that apartment. No crickets whistled and no frogs groaned. The wind did not come up through the floor. Only my brother's memory hung above my head in my single bedroom. I told myself that one day we would meet again, and I would show him that I had kept his slingshot.

My Centrelink money always ran out quickly. I was given four hundred dollars a fortnight; it cost me a hundred and seventy dollars a week to take care of my rent, and the leftover amount would get me a twelve-kilogram bag of rice, three kilograms of chicken, and that was pretty much it. I had to make my food last and have enough to pay for the train. I pushed harder to find a job but there was always the same answer: no.

Ms Li could see that my life was lonely. She had met me at school to see how I was going and I told her that no one wanted to hire me. She told me she would try to help and then she told me she was going to take me to a place where she hoped I would make friends. She said I had to find some fun and if I did, schooling and job-hunting wouldn't seem so hard. One Friday evening she picked me up and took me to a place called the Police-Citizens Youth Club (PCYC). I walked into a large building and the first thing I noticed was the smell of sweat. Pop music was blasting from the television hung on the wall and the room was full of lifting weights and other gym equipment. A bunch of old people were working out and some young guys were lifting weights that looked heavier than their own bodies. Nobody took any notice of us as we walked through into another space with soft multi-coloured mats stretched across the room. One side of the wall was covered by three big mirrors, and there was a boxing ring in the corner of the room. Next to the boxing ring was a big red-and-blue punching bag.

'You can come here to train, Isa,' Ms Li said.

The punching bag brought back memories. It reminded me of Moïse.

I started going to the club every spare moment I had. It felt comfortable, and the smell of sweat and the sound of my fists hitting the bag took me back to the afternoons in Bukavu, when I used to watch Moïse train. It cost me twelve dollars a week and it felt like money well spent. I didn't feel out of place here, and people let me be. Or they did until the evening an old man came up to me. His voice sounded excited and happy to see me despite not knowing me. I could barely keep up with all his questions.

'Hello, I'm Ryan. You're new here? Where are you from? Where do you live? What are you doing? I've trained so many young folks like you, you know, from Sudan. I like your people. You know, I used to do a thousand push-ups when I was your age ...'

From that night on, Ryan would always be there when I got to the club, and he would tell me how to lift my arm or to pull back at more of an angle before I hit the bag. Whether I liked it or not, I had made a friend.

ACT IV

chapter 11

a business card and a prayer

AFTER TWO YEARS IN AUSTRALIA I WAS STILL LEARNING new things every day. I hadn't heard from Nyota for over six months. The last time we'd spoken she'd given me the number of a new agency she'd found in the DRC that could help me find Moïse. I'd tried to call her and Auntie a few times, but the number just rang out. I felt abandoned, all alone in a big world.

Ms Li had found me a job in construction and so I had left Milpera. I had also moved into a small studio flat in Annerley, which was cheaper than the unit I had first lived in. It had a kitchenette down one end of a large room, and my bed down the other with a two-seater couch and a small table in the middle. It had a tiny bathroom with a shared toilet. I liked it because it meant I had more money to use to find Moïse. I was making a lot of expensive phone calls back to the agencies in the DRC.

The construction crew were a motley bunch, similar to the guys I attended language school with. There were big Islander guys, white guys, Asians and another African guy who was much older than me. There were even a few women, but nobody I could call a real friend.

My job included picking up the offcuts of timber on the floor, filling a wheelbarrow with them and then emptying that into a truck. It would take me more than fifty rounds to fill the back of the truck. We would work at different locations. Sometimes it would take us a week or two to complete a job, sometimes it would take us three months. I started work at eight in the morning and finished at four in the afternoon.

I had got myself into the routine of going for a run every morning before work. I'd head out early and sometimes I'd come across drunkards staggering home after a big night out. Some of them would want to pick a fight, but I'd ignore them and keep running. After work, I would go straight to the PCYC to do an evening session. I'd got to know the manager, Lachlan, and he would let me train even if I hadn't paid my weekly fee because I was waiting for my wages. He looked after the place and coached most people at the centre.

The construction work was very tiring. I would be stuck in those yellow-and-blue uniforms with steel-capped boots for the whole day, regardless of the heat. I liked having a job but I wasn't learning much. Anyone can pick up rubbish. But seeing people make something from bits of wood and steel made me want to build things. I asked Ms Li to help me find out what I would have to do to enrol in university. I still wanted to become a bridge builder. I didn't tell the crew I worked with, even though they would sometimes ask me what I wanted to do or what I was up to.

One day we were having a break under the shade of a big tree in a park next to our building site and the foreman stood up and said, 'Attention! Jayden here is turning eighteen, and y'all know what that means. His parents are away over the weekend, so we gotta show him how the big boys do it.'

Thommo, a big guy from Tonga, said, 'Yeah! We kick him in the balls and welcome him to adulthood? It works, bruh, that's what my brothers did to me when I turned eighteen. Got me a six-pack of condoms and locked me up in a room with a woman.'

Everyone laughed and the foreman high-fived Thommo. Everyone except Simone, who worked as a traffic controller, making it safe for the trucks to enter and leave the site. 'Why don't we just go to the park, have a barbecue there with a cold beer. That's an Australian thing, right?'

The foreman rubbed his face and ignored Simone. 'Rumour has it that our hero here is still stuck in Virginia, so we want him to lose that American accent. We're gonna book him a hotel, hook him up with a couple of pros … let him have a great time.'

No one asked Jayden what he wanted, and I watched his face turn redder and redder as the crew laughed and made fun of him. I didn't quite understand what was happening as the foreman passed around his hard hat and everyone put money in it. I leaned over to whisper to an African man, Leo, who was sitting next to me.

'Is Jayden American?'

'No, he's a virgin, so they're gonna hook him up with some girls.'

'What's a pro?' I was learning new Australian words every day.

'A pro is another word for a prostitute. Somebody who sleeps with people for cash.'

As I put money in the hat and went back to work, I tried not to think of the girl who was made to sleep with me for her life.

⤺

Ms Li set up a meeting for me with a student advisor at Queensland University of Technology to discuss the possibility of me enrolling.

I was still in my yellow-and-blue workwear and boots when I arrived at the administration office, where the receptionist gave me a form to fill in and an English proficiency test to do right in front of her.

After I was done, I was called into a room by a man who looked young, maybe in his thirties. His hair was tied at the back like a woman. He didn't say much as his eyes were fixed on the forms I had just completed. After about five minutes' silence he said, 'So, Eezea … I hope I got that right?'

'You say it "Eesah Alakey",' I replied.

'Thank you. So, Eezah, what makes you want to study engineering?'

I didn't know what to say, so I stayed quiet.

'I understand you did some studies in Kenya and spent some time at Milpera but, it's not enough, Eezah. Engineering is very competitive. It requires a high level of English, even via the alternative-entry route. Judging from your English proficiency test, I don't think you're quite ready for it just yet. I suggest you go home, work on your English, have a bit of a think about what you really want to do. Some people go to TAFE to do a certificate or a diploma before applying for a tertiary degree. That's how you can improve your language and you can transfer your TAFE credit to university.'

He paused and then added, 'I hope you didn't get the idea of engineering because of your parents. You'd be surprised how many people want to study engineering because their mother thought they were good at building Lego. We already have too many bridges on the Brisbane River.'

'Back home we have too many rivers but no bridges. Just alligators and fish,' I responded.

'We don't have that many alligators here, mate. Just a couple of bull sharks.' He laughed and then went on. 'But, like I said, if this is what you really want to do, then go home and think about your options.'

I didn't want to hear what he was telling me. Maybe he didn't want to help me achieve my dreams. That night, the darkness fell faster than normal. My house got much colder than usual.

After dinner, I called the DRC to talk to the aid-agency guy who was helping me find Moïse.

'Sorry, Isa, we've hit a brick wall here,' the man said. 'You'll have to try something else. Can I suggest a man I know who lives in Goma, a private investigator? He has a great record of finding missing persons. But he won't be free, like me; he would want to be paid. A lot of money. If you want, I can reach out to him.'

I didn't care how much it cost if I found Moïse.

It took him a week to get back to me, and just as he said, the private investigator wanted money. I was earning much more than I had received from Centrelink but it still wasn't enough. That night ended with me kneeling on the floor next to my bed with my arms folded. I said a prayer just as my mother had taught me.

The next night, I went to the PCYC to participate in an amateur boxing competition. Ryan was there and he told anyone who would listen how proud he was to coach me. Ryan would always cheer for me when I was in the ring.

Give me instructions. Not that I followed them all, but he was always proud of my wins.

There were about fifty casually dressed blokes and a few women in the crowd, sitting on folding chairs around the red boxing ring. My first fight was against a musclebound white guy who was about thirty but looked in his forties. Lachlan was our referee. He had his work cut out for him keeping up with us. I ducked and weaved like a maniac, trying to stay away from the guy's jabs. Ryan shouted out and cheered for me. 'Go for the head, Eezah, the head!'

I was doing the opposite of what Ryan was telling me to do. I was all over the shop, throwing a combination of body shots, swinging and punching like there was no tomorrow. I didn't see the small tracksuited woman in her fifties with short grey curly hair and glasses watching me like a hawk. She was sitting at the back of the gym. My opponent was good but I knocked him out in the third round.

As I walked out of the change room after the fight, Lachlan was standing by the doorway talking to the lady and another man. I stopped close to them to take a sip from my water bottle.

'I told you he was something else, didn't I?' I heard Lachlan say.

'Yeah, a thug,' the man responded. 'He fights dirty and all, no doubt about that.'

'The guy's a machine. He just keeps going no matter what they throw at him,' Lachlan said.

'How long has he been boxing?' the lady asked.

'He turned up two years ago, but he doesn't talk much and that's his problem. Very uncommunicative. So, I don't know how long he's been boxing. But you can't deny his talent. Since he's been here, he's had ten fights for ten wins. All knockouts. He's a one-off. I can't get anyone in the ring with him anymore. They know they can't beat him.'

The lady looked over, caught my eye and nodded. I was embarrassed that I had been caught listening. I just wanted to get moving but Lachlan turned and saw me.

'Here he is: Isa Alaki, undefeated champ of all the PCYCs. I want you to meet Lucy Clarke, Isa.'

The man next to Lucy walked away.

'Hello,' I said.

'That was one heck of a knockout back there,' Lucy said.

'Lucy runs Clarke's Boxing Gym in West End, Isa. Best gym in Brisbane. World class. All the top pros train there. You heard of Des Clarke? Never mind. Des is Lucy's late husband. Three-time Australian heavyweight champion, back in the nineties,' Lachlan said.

Lucy stuck her hand out to me. 'Here is my business card. The address is on the back. You should drop by the gym sometime. Come check it out. We're open twenty-four seven.'

I thanked her and said goodbye. I remembered my father telling me about these types of people: they are never motivated towards an individual; all they want is to use you and toast you around town. Once they have taken advantage of you, they move on to the next person. And why were women who slept with men for money training at this gym?

I went home, my jacket pulled tight and my sports bag in my hands. I was welcomed by loud music from partying neighbours who lived across from my room. I opened my door, emptied my pockets and threw Lucy's business card in the wastepaper basket before lying down on my narrow bed. The music wouldn't let me close my eyes even though my body was exhausted. The voices from the party sounded like screaming children, men and women. Their feet stomping on the floor sounded like running and dropped grenades. Every time the bass sounded, it shook the ceiling like an exploding bomb. I folded my arms to thank God for another day, but the music was bringing me misery. So, I got up and logged on to the Internet on my phone to search for my brother. I tried all the possibilities. *Moïse Alaki, Alaki Ombele's son. Moïse Alaki Bukavu. Moïse Alaki child soldier.* Nothing came up. So, I tried on Facebook and Twitter. Just like Google, they didn't bring up any results. I tried to call Nyota but there was no answer. When the music stopped I finally drifted into an uneasy sleep, dreaming that my brother was with me, and then waking to the nightmare of knowing he wasn't.

chapter 12

not my world

I WAS WORKING BY DAY, TRAINING BY NIGHT AND GOING to English classes at TAFE. The class was a lot like Milpera but now I could understand what was being said and didn't feel quite so out of place. There were a mixed bunch of adults: Asians, Africans, South Americans. At nineteen, I was the youngest in the class. My first day at TAFE was no different from the first time I went to Milpera. Our teacher, Mrs Fran, who looked younger than some of the students in the class, was mousy with sensible shoes. She would always pace between the desks.

'Okay, we're going to go around the class and I want you to tell us what you did over the weekend. Name first, because we have some new faces in the class.'

'Hi, my name is Isabella Marianna, I am from Brazil. On the weekend I watched a movie with my girlfriends. I love movies with African-Americans in them. The way they talk with their American accent and when they take their clothes off …'

The whole class laughed, except for me. I was mortified.

'Okay, Isabella, we get the idea. Who's next?' said Mrs Fran, still pacing between our tables, looking this way and that waiting for the next person to speak.

An elderly African man put his hand up. 'Hello, my name is Abdul Kon, I am from Sudan and I have seven children. I take some of my children to watch Queensland Roar game against Melbourne City.'

'Good, Abdul, excellent. Now, anybody else?' Mrs Fran continued to walk around, pointing to the Iraqi boys who sat at the back of the classroom. They didn't have anything to say. She then pointed to me, sitting in the third row. The whole class turned to look at me.

'Come on, what's your name?'

'Isa.'

'Isa who?'

'Isa Smith.' I don't know why I didn't say my family name. Why was I denying who I was?

The whole class started laughing.

'Okay, Isa Smith, what did you do over the weekend?'

'Nothing much.'

'Come on, you can do better than that! We have a dinner get-together on Friday night down in the Valley.' She returned to the front of the class. 'It's great for you to come and socialise. Your attendance will be marked as ten percent towards your final marks.'

I didn't know what else she wanted me to tell her. But she moved on to the next person and I zoned out to a place where no other person could reach me.

A zone where my mind was trained to eliminate the rest of the world. It was a zone of comfort and despair. A zone where animals flew and birds crawled on their stomachs and only the toughest survived. A zone of horrors and atrocities. A zone where the world was eternally red. Where children no longer mattered. Where men and women were no different. A zone where the family name Alaki was not worthy.

It was the only place I truly felt I existed. But it was a place I wanted to leave. I just didn't know how.

⤙

ON THE FRIDAY evening of the get-together, I put on my best jeans with a clean and ironed T-shirt, ready for the night out. I had taken my time to get ready. I stood in the shower and let the water run hard, scrubbing the day's dirt and sweat off my body, and then combed my hair and rubbed the marks off my shoes. By the time I was dressed and closing my door I was running late, so I got on a city express train. As it approached South Bank station, an announcement came over the speakers telling us that all trains to the city were delayed due to trackwork. I got off the train and made my way to the ferry on the bank of the river. As I got to the wharf, I saw a few young African teenagers in line ahead of me. As they went to board, they were stopped because they didn't have the ferry fare.

As I got to the front of the line the man in charge thought I was part of the teenage crew and told me I couldn't get on. I took my pass out to show him, but he didn't care. All he saw was that I was African and the people ahead of me were also African and they didn't have tickets, so we were all barred from the ferry. I didn't argue; I knew there was no point. I started running towards the footbridge and finally, sweaty, hot and not feeling quite right, I made it to the restaurant. All the other students were there, laughing, and it seemed to me they were having a good time. Nobody noticed me. I still didn't feel right, so I turned around and headed for the closest train station.

As I walked by the crowded restaurants it seemed everyone was having a good time with friends or family. It made me feel even worse. I walked to the nearest McDonald's and bought a burger, then walked to Brunswick Street. The streets were packed with people going about their night, some adults and other young ones. All different races.

Most people walked in pairs, stepping to the rhythm of the buskers at the corners of the city streets, who were playing beautiful music. Sometimes their footsteps danced to the reggae music that came through the windows of an overcrowded pub. The whole city seemed illuminated and the different coloured street lights made everything look vibrant and hid the dirty and dark corners. The night felt electric. I watched a group of four young boys riding their skateboards, doing jumps and tricks off gutters and seats. A group of young African girls and their boyfriends passed by on the opposite side of the road, headed towards the city. Among them was a boy with a radio, blasting African music as he walked along.

A young white girl in tiny shorts and high stilettos smiled at me from the other side of the road. I stopped to look at her but a bus came and blocked my view. When the bus left, the girl had disappeared.

I kept walking. Not far from the railway station I heard screams coming from a laneway behind a nightclub. I saw a woman stumbling towards me, a man was chasing her and they were both weaving drunkenly. He raised an acoustic guitar that he was carrying and then crashed it down on her head.

I ran towards them and pushed the guy away from the woman and tried to grab his guitar. The woman fell to the ground while the guy started to swing his guitar at me, screaming, 'Fuck off, you black bastard! Fuck off!'

I knocked the guy down to the ground, wrenched his guitar off him and then tried to help the woman up. She pushed me away as she staggered to her feet.

'Why don't you mind your own business, you black cunt! You heard him, fuck off. Why don't you go back to where you fucking came from, you fuckin' cockhead!'

A crowd had gathered and a couple of teenagers had their phones out, recording. The girlfriend started to scream, standing over her boyfriend, who was still lying on the ground. 'He's fucking killed him! Someone call the cops.'

The boyfriend started to get up, and I took off without looking back. All I could hear was that woman's words. *Mind your own business, you black cunt.*

Once I was sure no one was following me, I stopped. My hands were shaking, as if they were laid down on top of a washing machine. My stomach heaved and I wanted to cry. I slowly walked to the train station, oblivious to anyone or anything else that went on around me. I got on the train to Annerley and sat with my head down until I arrived at my stop. I didn't dare look up, look at anyone's face. My mind was no longer with me. My thoughts were trying to catch up with the rest of me. I slowly walked from the station to my flat and when I got inside I went down on my knees at my bedside, with my hands folded, and gave thanks I made it to my home safely.

Sun past point midpoint.
I am walking down the track.
1400 hours.
Flames flow deep from the side of these dark signs.
Wisdom glows deeper beneath the concrete on which we
*   pound our feet.*
The dark nights rise when the sun falls.

Where there is light, no darkness should prosper.
Man has brought darkness into the light.
Making you fall to a deeper damnation where your
voice can no longer scream louder than you can
stand. I can't understand these languages.
The light glows when cats crawl beneath stools, climbing
tools with their sharp claws.
It's not my world. It's definitely not my world when
frozen waters run above your mind and blind your
vision.
I see butterflies. They fly beneath red roses and sing
songs of wisdom.
Songs of grace. Their emotions are flirtatious but their
actions are despicable.
It's not my world.
It cannot be my world when the broken receive the
highest condemnation.
No reactions from men who stand for what they believe
in. Cowards judge every other man.
It cannot be my world when black always appears
inferior to the rest.
No excuse but excuse me when my language is
insensible. Incomprehensible.

I was taught by a man who was taught by another man
from a place different from mine.
My mind is frozen. Frozen deeper under muddy creeks
where frogs lay their heads. Broken shells grow on
my nails from the hatred we are fed by people who
don't matter.
It's not my world when children watch their mothers
die from the hands of their own brothers who
repeatedly tell them I love you.
It's not my world when children become men and men
behave like wild animals, feeding on weak minds.
It cannot be my world.

⌒

THE NEXT MONDAY evening, I went back to the Multicultural Development Association to see Ms Li. I still had my hard hat and blue-and-yellow work uniform. The receptionist asked me to take a seat on the sofa and said Ms Li would attend to me as soon as possible. Moments later, Ms Li emerged from one of the rooms and asked me to follow her.

'Here, take a seat.'

She left me and then returned with two cups of tea and slid them onto the table. 'I didn't know how many sugars you take so, I brought you these,' she said, putting some small paper packets on the table next to my cup.

'Thank you,' I responded.

'I'm really sorry it didn't work out with the university, Isa. But I think you should be practising your English more with writing and reading. Then you can reapply. How is the English class going?'

'Okay.'

'Just okay? Are you getting along with your classmates?'

I didn't know what to tell Ms Li, so I just nodded.

'Good! The more you socialise, the easier it will get for you. The only way your English is going to improve is by talking to people. Reading newspapers, magazines and books.'

She handed me a magazine. 'Read this.'

While Ms Li continued talking, a girl approached her desk. She looked to be in her mid-twenties and she had long dark hair. She was incredibly beautiful.

'Hello,' she greeted Ms Li and smiled at me. 'This must be Heezah,' she said.

'It's Isa,' I replied.

'It's a pleasure to meet you, Isa, I am Trinity. Did Ms Li give you the invitation to the meet and greet?'

'Not yet,' Ms Li said. 'Thanks for the reminder. We're having a meet and greet for the new arrivals from the DRC next Saturday week. I think it would be great for you too if you can make it.'

I left Ms Li's office but Trinity's smile was still in the back of my mind. I liked that picture in my head.

It didn't take long to get to the PCYC and soon I was on the punching bag. It swung from side to side from the heavy hits I delivered. Jab-jab-duck. Jab-jab-duck. Sweat spilled down my chest, flooding the floor like a rainy day. Only Ryan's voice was audible above the rhythmic hits. Giving instructions for how to punch properly or how to move. Sometimes he would do the same thing my brother used to do: count up from one but never go past four. One. One two. One, one two three. Ryan told me that he used to punch the bag until it split open. That he used to do a hundred chin-ups and had amazing biceps when he was a younger man.

I ignored Ryan and kept hitting the bag.

'Your girlfriend is here,' Ryan said. I stopped and looked up to see the grey-haired woman who'd given me her business card walking towards me. 'Ask her if she's got a friend,' Ryan said with a big smile on his face.

'Hello again, friend,' Lucy shouted over the music. 'I was waiting for your call.'

I said hello.

'How about dinner, aye?' Lucy said as she offered her hand. 'I know a good place where they serve good food.'

I had a feeling she wasn't someone who took no for an answer. I looked at her hand.

'Okay.'

Lucy drove us past Woolloongabba to the other side of town in her old Merc.

'Everyone says you are good, Isa. I could see that the other day. I think you could get better, though. A lot better. But you are not going to get better staying at the PCYC. You need to train in a good environment and surround yourself with pros. When you train with pros, you'll see it for yourself.

'You don't talk much, do you?'

After a while we hit an industrial area, with the city skyscrapers still visible in the distance, and drove up to a cluster of down-at-heel shops selling tattoos, kebabs, pizza and taxation advice. Above them all was a huge cut-out of two boxers squaring off on a billboard advertising Clarke's Boxing Gym, Open 24/7. Lucy turned down a narrow driveway running beside the shops. She parked her car in a small gravel parking area around the back of the buildings, alongside an outdoor training area. A rundown boxing ring was in the middle of a slightly shaded area. The shade cloth was secured to the side of a small apartment at the bottom of some stairs. Above the ring was a digital clock.

'This is where we train in summer. Ten minutes out here is worth half an hour inside,' Lucy said.

Next to the ring was a busted-up punching bag that looked about fifty years old. The bag was hanging from a rusty metal chain hooked onto a pole cemented into the ground. Nearby was an old basketball hoop and a huge truck tyre the size of a big table. The tyre would reach my height if stood up. In a pile to the side were a stack of rusty weights. Everything looked shabby.

Lucy signalled for me to follow her inside. We went up the rickety wooden stairs and in through the door at the top of the apartment.

Inside, loud pop music was blasting from the two TV sets up high above the mirrors. The room smelled of fresh rubber and protein powder. A table full of gold championship medals and trophies was sitting to the right of the main entrance. The place looked old but still sparkly. Unlike at the PCYC, the mirrors were clean with no smears or blackened watermarks.

A couple of girls were hard at work kickboxing in the corner of the room, next to five brand new punching bags. I couldn't help but wonder if they were the prostitutes Lucy had been talking about.

Two heavily tattooed young boxers were sparring in a red boxing ring at the back of the gym. One white guy and one Indigenous guy; they wore matching sleeveless shirts, boxing shoes, big socks and strappings around their ankles and fists. They were going hard. The sweat ran down their tattooed shoulders and bulging biceps. A man was pacing around them barking instructions. Next to the main entrance was a small reception desk and a few brand new weights laid out perfectly on a small shelf. A few bikes, chin-up bars and other pieces of well-maintained gym equipment were grouped on the other side of the room.

To the left of the boxing ring was a small lounge area with a vending machine, a pool table, two couches and another television. Behind one of the couches were many pairs of boxing gloves, all in different colours. The rest of the walls were filled with images of boxers. Right at the back of the gym was a small office with a big glass window featuring another sign that read 'Clarke's Gym'.

Two air-conditioning systems were working overtime to keep the place cool as everyone trained. A few young men were working out with weights and machines. They all looked seriously fit and focused. None of them were paying attention to us as Lucy showed me around.

'Do you like my gym?' she asked. 'Do you like my pictures? They are my inspiration. If you work hard, that could be you. But you must have a dream. Unless you have a dream, you can never achieve anything. Before you take a step, you must have a purpose and you must learn respect. What is your purpose?'

I didn't know what she wanted to hear from me but she didn't give me a chance to reply anyway.

'My husband and I started this place twenty years ago, after he'd retired from boxing. That's him right there.' She pointed to a framed photograph on the wall of a boxer standing on the ropes and raising a championship belt into the air.

'Des Clarke,' she said. 'Everything I know about boxing, I learned from Des. House of Dreams, he wanted to call it. That's what it was in those days. A house of dreams. Our boxers won every state and national title we could get our hands on. We had everyone who was anyone lining up to train with us or even get a shot. It's a bit quieter now.'

The man who had been coaching the two tattooed guys walked up to us, and I recognised him as the man who'd been with Lucy the first time I talked to her. He ignored me and said to Lucy, 'You have visitors,' pointing to a couple of men in suits entering from the main door.

'Sorry, Isa, this won't take long. Make yourself at home. If you have any questions, just ask Tim.'

I watched as she hurried over to the two men with a tight smile on her face and her hand stretched out. She led the suits to the little office down the back of the gym, shutting the door behind her as she entered and then wound the blinds down.

'We haven't been properly introduced. I'm Tim.'

I focused on his face again and held out my hand. 'I remember you.'

'So, why do you want to box?'

'To get better.'

Tim asked me about my technique and what I liked to do best for training.

As we continued talking, Lucy led the suits out of the office to the gym's entrance, and then came back to us.

'How long have you been in Brisbane?' Tim said.

'Two years.'

'Still new. How was the flight?'

'I thought I was going to die. They gave me this long thing! Saus … saw …?'

'You mean a sausage? You'll be eating a lot of them here,' Lucy said.

'What is it made of? I like heavy food like fufu.'

'We have better food than your fufo,' Lucy said.

'It's fufu.'

'Yeah, yeah! We'll find you Weet-Bix and you'll be fine.'

'What's Wit bix?'

'You've been here two years and you don't know what Weet-Bix are? They're brick-looking things that you mix with milk until they become mush.'

'And people eat this?'

'Yeah, it's actually quite delicious if you put honey on it.'

I looked over to the two girls kickboxing and asked, 'Are those girls the prostitutes?'

'Mate, you better not let them hear you call them that!'

When I told Tim that I'd learned what a pro was, he started laughing. 'A pro can also mean a professional athlete, and you better not mix them up.' He was still laughing as he led me down to the basement where more framed posters of famous boxers lined the walls of two training rooms. Both were empty with mats laid out perfectly on the floor. The first room had climbing frames built onto one side of the wall with big nets hanging across the other side. A bench was set in the middle. Similarly, the second room was empty with only a few more nets hanging from the top of the walls.

'We use this place for kickboxing or any highly physical exercises,' Tim said. 'Make sure you take off your shoes before you go inside.'

The rooms smelled like fresh rubber, like nobody had ever been in there. At least not for a very long time.

We went back up to the main gym where the two boxers in the ring were taking a break. One of them was in the office with Lucy, while the other was having a drink. With the blinds up again, I could see that Lucy was counting money and then handing it over to him. The man came out with his face glowing as if he had seen God. Lucy followed him out. 'They make some good money, these boys – and that was only his third professional fight,' she said to me while Tim jumped back into the ring.

'Anyways, Isa, you're welcome here, any day, any time. We're always open. Twenty-four seven.'

I wandered around a bit to take another good look at the place before I headed home. My mind was ticking over. Maybe my prayers had just been answered.

chapter 13

this isn't war

Finally I had a little bit of hope. Maybe the skills my brother taught me were going to help me find him.

I called the private investigator in Goma to ask what he could do.

'I'm going to need the name of the missing person. The place you last saw him. His age. Everything about him. Build, height, any facial characteristics or any distinguishing marks. Anything that would help me identify him. And I'm going to need ten thousand dollars to do the job.'

'Ten thousand dollars?'

'Yeah. Will that be a problem?'

'No. No. No problem.' But it was a problem. I didn't know where I was going to get that much money.

'The sooner you can send through the money; the sooner I can get going on it.'

I asked him some more questions and he asked me lots more about Moïse. I could hear him typing up my words as I spoke.

After ten minutes he said he had all he needed to get started and he gave me his bank details and we hung up.

The three thousand dollars I had saved in the shoebox under my bed wasn't going to be enough to start with. Somehow I had to get the rest. That night I kneeled beside my bed and said another prayer.

First thing at work the next morning I approached my foreman and asked to talk to him in private. He took me into the site office, which was a temporary tin shed at the side of the block, and I told him I was looking for my brother back home and needed seven thousand dollars. I had worked out a plan where I could pay him back in instalments on a weekly basis until it was all paid off. My foreman shook his head and told me he couldn't do that, so I asked him if he could give me more work. Maybe I could start earlier or work later?

'I'm sorry, Isa, but we can't give overtime to casuals. Company rules. But tell you what: how about an advance on next week's pay? Would that help?'

'No, but thank you,' I answered.

'Sorry, mate. I wish I could help but there's just no way.'

That afternoon I went back to Clarke's Gym straight after work. I pressed the buzzer until one of the girls let me in.

Tim was in the ring with the same two guys as the day before. Lucy was in her office tending to her papers, so I knocked on the open door.

'What can I do for you, young man?' Lucy said.

'What do I have to do to become a professional boxer?'

Lucy stared at me in surprise. She took off her small glasses and placed them on the desk.

'If you're serious about this, then I can help you. But it takes time, son.'

'I want to do it, but I don't have a lot of time.'

'Well, let's get started now, shall we?' She walked me over to the ring and said, 'Johnny, do you want to square out with young Isa here? It's gonna be fun.'

'Okay, sure! I'm gonna enjoy this.'

Tim didn't look so happy and he walked up to Lucy with a face I couldn't read. 'This is a stupid idea.'

'It's just a try-out, okay?'

'You think he's gonna save us? He's not, you know. No one can.'

Lucy turned her back on Tim and grabbed a pair of gloves. She passed them to me and helped me make sure they were taped on properly. I stepped into the ring, and Johnny walked over to his corner. Tim stepped inside too.

Lucy pulled a whistle on a string out of her pocket and looped it over her head. She gave us all a nod and then blew the whistle hard to get us started.

Johnny was good; the best fighter I had ever faced. He was quick on his feet and landed a few punches on me, but he was not protecting himself. I could see his vulnerability and took advantage of it. I knocked him down with a power punch. As he staggered to his feet, I knocked him down again and then again. I hit him hard, really hard, over and over until he wasn't able to get up. I continued punching him. I didn't hear Lucy blowing her whistle.

'Hey, hey! Tim, stop him!' Lucy shouted.

While Tim was trying to pull me away from Johnny, Lucy was watching it all from the sidelines. When I looked over, her face showed a mixture of emotions. She seemed horrified, but at the same time fascinated by what she had just witnessed. Blood dripped down Johnny's face. Tim helped him stand and steadied him, before taking him to the men's change room. Blood had pooled on the mats in the ring.

'What the hell was that?' Lucy said to me before rushing off after Johnny.

A minute later Lucy was back. 'What were you thinking? You guys are on the same team! If you wanna train here, don't you ever fight like that again. You understand? Otherwise, I'll show you the door. This isn't war, mate, it's a game where you shake hands at the end of it. You'll never get anywhere fighting like that!'

I was mortified. I took off the gloves and threw them on the floor, jumped over the ropes, took my bag and headed for the stairs. They all condemned me with their eyes as I walked out of the gym. I had no friends here.

As soon as I got home, I found a message from the private investigator. He was asking when I could send the money so he could start searching for Moïse. The prayer wasn't helping and I had no idea what I was going to do.

I tried to call Nyota but there was no answer. I was worried that something had happened to Auntie and frustrated that I couldn't contact her or Nyota. That night I lay in bed turning over in my mind what I could do. I had no answers and no one to talk to. I was completely alone.

⌐

THE NEXT FEW days, I felt like I was sleepwalking. I couldn't shake the sadness that was heavy on me. I felt listless; all I could manage was getting to work, then I'd go home and sleep. When I slept I stopped thinking, and even if the nightmares came, I didn't care. I couldn't eat, didn't want to talk to anyone. Ms Li called to make sure I was coming to the next get-together. I tried to say no but she wouldn't accept it. I didn't have the energy to argue. It was easier to say yes. She told me she would pick me up, so I couldn't back out.

That Friday evening I dressed in my best jeans and ironed a shirt. All I wanted was to stay home and sleep some more, but I made myself wait outside. I was just about to go back inside and lock the door when I saw Ms Li's car turn into my street. As I jumped into the passenger seat she said, 'I know you didn't want to come, Isa, but I am very glad you changed your mind.' She told me about the new arrivals from the DRC and I realised that someone might have seen or have news of Moïse. Ms Li kept talking but I didn't listen properly, I was suddenly hopeful that I might get some information and not have to pay the private investigator. For the first time since I had been in Clarke's Gym I didn't have a pain in my chest.

Moorooka Community Hall was buzzing with laughter and conversation as we walked in. Everyone was talking at once in a cacophony of Congolese languages – Swahili, Lingala and some French here and there. Most of the Congolese women were in brightly coloured dresses and elaborate headscarves while the men were mostly in suits or dashikis. Most of the children were in their Sunday best and some looked like miniature replicas of their parents. At the front of the hall a group of people were being led by a pastor, singing hymns beneath a big banner reading 'MDA – Multicultural Development Association'. I lost Ms Li almost straightaway and a bit later I saw her moving between people, talking and shaking hands. Then I saw Trinity. She was standing with an old lady, chatting and smiling. As soon as she saw me, she lifted her hand up and waved as she started walking towards me with her hand out.

'*Jambo!*' she said. '*Furaha ku honana. Siku juwa wewe kuja.*' It was a bad attempt at Swahili. I think she wanted to say, 'Hi, I'm happy to see you. I didn't think you'd make it.' I started laughing.

'What's so funny?'

'My English is better than your Swahili.'

She started laughing too. 'Ms Li told me you've been here for two years, so how come I've never seen you at a get-together before?'

'These things are not my cup of coffee.'

'You mean "cup of tea"?'

'Do I?'

'I don't know, you tell me! You're supposedly the English expert. So, you don't like hanging out with your own people?'

'Not with any people.'

'I'm only here because I'm working. What's your excuse?'

'I'm looking for someone.'

'Who?'

'Family.'

While Trinity and I were deep in our conversation, Ms Li appeared.

'I hope you two haven't been speaking in Swahili. Isa needs to practise his English. Go talk to people, Isa, and remember to use your English. Practise, practise.'

Trinity rolled her eyes as Ms Li pushed me over to a group of people. I went around in circles asking everyone where they were from and how long they had been away from the DRC. Unfortunately, no one had come from Goma or Bukavu, so I had no luck finding anyone who knew Moïse. I stayed right to the end, making sure I spoke to everyone. Whenever I caught Trinity's eye she would smile at me, and I liked knowing she was in the room. But when it was time to leave I said goodbye quickly. The heavy sadness was back and I needed to think of another plan.

Without money, I had no chance of finding my brother. I went home and it was another long night but in the darkness of the early morning I heard my father's voice. *'Where there is a trail, there is a way that leads home.'*

I would find that trail and find my way home to Moïse.

chapter 14

hold the dream

ON THAT SATURDAY I WOKE EARLY AND THE HEAT OF THE day had already wrapped itself around everything. The sun felt like it was burning through my T-shirt as I waited for the bus to take me to Clarke's Gym in West End. It was the only option I had unless I wanted to rob someone. But I was an Alaki and we are honourable people. I'd told myself after the day that Auntie was attacked that I would never steal again.

I walked into the coolness of the air-conditioned gym. Lucy and Tim were there, working with a couple of young boxers in the ring. They saw me but continued working as if they hadn't. The coolness in the air wasn't just from the air-conditioner. I started to walk to the ring and Lucy climbed over the ropes to head me off, nodding to Tim as she did.

'I want you to train me,' I said, not giving her a chance to speak.

'Are you serious?'

I nodded.

'You have to have control if you're ever gonna become a good fighter.' I heard anger in her voice and I looked down at the floor. 'I can teach you technique but I can't teach you how to control your mind. You look at me when I am talking to you. You hear me?'

'Yes,' I said as I lifted my head up and looked her in the eyes. She stared straight back at me, not showing any kindness.

'Do you want to be a champion? Yes or no?'

'Yes!'

'I don't want to waste my time. You're gonna have to prove to me you can control yourself. That you can listen and take orders. Understand?'

I nodded.

'This is my gym and I have rules that everyone around here follows. No drugs, no alcohol and no street fighting. And you must learn respect. Can you do that?'

'Yes,' I said. Lucy looked at me and then over to Tim. He was shaking his head but there was a smile on his face.

'Good, we'll start tomorrow. Now get out of here!'

I GOT HOME and listened to the music of Luambo Makiadi, a famous Congolese artist from the sixties. It was the music my father used to play. My father said the old music had more meaning than the modern popular music that Rita liked so much. He used to say that music in those days talked about real issues that people went through every day. I didn't agree with him back then. And Rita used to yell and tell him he was old-fashioned. But now it was the only music I liked. It reminded me of my father. And of home.

After a long day, it was time to put my body to rest and to prepare for what was to come. I said my prayers and stretched myself in my narrow bed. The night fell with peace.

The next day I showed up at the gym, where I found the same two suited men along with three other people wandering around taking pictures of the place and making notes on their phones. Tim was putting up a poster on the far wall advertising an upcoming fight at the Mansfield Tavern in Mount Gravatt. Lucy was sitting on a seat beside the ring and watching the suits constantly. She didn't look happy. But then she saw me and smiled.

'When can I fight there?' I asked, pointing to the poster as she walked towards me with a pair of gloves.

'When you're ready,' she replied.

'I'm ready.'

Tim walked up, ignored me, and said to Lucy, 'That's crazy talk. It's too soon. We both know he needs to get some amateur fights under his belt before he jumps in a ring with an experienced fighter. His dream could end before it even starts.'

Lucy stared at Tim and said, 'We'll teach him what he needs to know.'

While Lucy and Tim continued talking, one of the suits came up to her. He extended his hand but Lucy ignored it.

'Thank you for that. We'll get going now,' he said, brushing his hand over his hair as if he hadn't just been dissed.

'Next time, why don't you call first before showing up uninvited, huh?' Lucy said. The men couldn't get out of the place fast enough. I didn't know what was going on but I knew that Lucy didn't like having those men there.

Lucy threw the pair of gloves to me while Tim picked up two pads that had been leaning against the wall and signalled me to follow him inside the ring.

'I think you know the basics, but the basics are what help you win a fight, if done correctly,' Tim said. With one of his hands raised, he showed me what to do.

'When I say one, you hit once. When I say one, two, you hit twice.'

We started doing the exercise. Tim would call out numbers from one to three, repeatedly. But then, the one-two didn't necessarily mean hitting it twice. Lucy stood in the ring and explained the purpose of each combination as we practised over and over. His combos would be: jab-jab; uppercut; jab; slip-slip; jab-jab. Then he would call the combo in numbers. For instance, he would call one-two, which is generally jab-right cross and is the basic combination that everyone learns or naturally knows before they even start boxing. The fast jab catches your opponent off guard and the right cross knocks his head off.

The next combo Tim called was one-one-two: jab-jab-cross. Lucy broke down this combination and said it was used to trick your opponent. The one-one-two works when your opponent might be expecting you to throw a one-two combo. Your second jab has a greater chance of surprising an opponent and opening the way for your right hand. She told me it works much better if you're a southpaw or a left-handed fighter who leads with the right hand. The one-one-two combo was also good if you felt your opponent was waiting for your right cross so they could throw a counter punch. Instead of throwing a normal one-two, Lucy told me I should throw endless jabs to test an opponent's defence until he slipped up and then I could put a right cross directly in his face, leaving him needing critical medical attention. Tim tried not to laugh at that.

'No time for laughing,' Lucy said. 'Back to it! And listen up, Isa.'

'I'm listening,' I said.

'Okay, well, a one-two-three or a jab-cross-left hook allows you to move fluently. The shift of your body weight when you throw the right hand naturally sets up the left hook. The left hook comes after your right cross and can cause massive damage to your opponent. You can aim it high at their jaw or low on their body. Either way, the left hook is very dangerous regardless of whether or not your right cross lands.'

Lucy kept talking as Tim took me through more and more combinations.

'You must learn to adapt to your opponent, Isa,' Lucy said.

It was like I was taken into a zone. I was in a trance every time I threw a punch. The skills my brother taught me were coming through in a different form. All the survival skills I learned as a child soldier were coming to the fore. I was shifting and adapting, ready for anything.

'In the ring, it's you against yourself,' Lucy said. 'Don't let your opponent manipulate your mind. Don't lose focus and give your opponent a chance.'

Tim ramped it up, punching me with the pads. He was hitting harder than I expected. I was sweating more and slowing down. My feet were getting tired and my body was shutting down. But he kept pushing harder and harder.

'Block out the pain. It's a sign of weakness,' Lucy said. 'When you get tired, your opponent will find a way to knock you out cold and you'll lose!' Lucy shouted.

Even though I knew what she was saying was true, my body was giving up on me. It was the toughest training session I'd ever had. Nothing like the jab-jab-duck my brother taught me.

Finally Tim dropped the pads down and Lucy threw me a bottle of water. I drank thirstily and then Lucy said, 'Right, you ready?'

'Yes,' I said.

She called a guy named Richard in to spar with me. We touched gloves and started sparring.

'Hold the dream, Isa, hold the dream.'

I thought of Moïse. I was holding on to him.

chapter 15

fight night

RICHARD AND I WERE JOGGING ALONGSIDE THE BRISBANE River, making our way up to the Story Bridge and then back to West End. It was late afternoon and there were a lot of people around. We had to weave our way through slow-walking groups and kids on bikes. We were taking it slowly, warming up our bodies for later that night. I'd been training full-on with Lucy and Tim for six weeks and I was fitter and sharper than I had ever been. If I wasn't at work or at class I was in the gym. After every session I asked when I could have a professional fight, and Lucy replied every time, 'When I think you're ready – and you're not ready yet.'

Four days before I'd asked the same question expecting the usual response, but this time Lucy had said, 'You're ready.' She told me she'd booked me for the next professional card at the Mansfield Tavern.

Those last four days had passed slowly, and now I tried to settle my nerves as I ran next to Richard. We'd been teamed up as sparring partners and I had got to like his quiet intensity. He was fighting his third bout that night and was making a name for himself.

I was glad he was with me as I walked into the venue. The place was packed. There were twenty decorated tables arranged around the ring. I had never seen that many people at a fight before. It was very different to the PCYC. I saw Lachlan and Ryan and waved.

A blue boxing ring was in the middle of the room surrounded by a cheering crowd of about 150 people. Lucy saw us and waved us over. She pointed out the change room and told us to go and get sorted, and that Tim was waiting for us in there. I walked past three eager men sitting at the table closest to the ring and saw the sheets of paper in front of them. They were judges. I turned away; looking at them made me nervous. I heard my name and glanced back. Thommo and a few of my workmates were there, cheering me on. That made me feel good but even more nervous.

Before I knew it, the announcer was in the ring calling me up.

'Welcome to our third preliminary fight, ladies and gentlemen. In this bout, we have Isa Alaki from Clarke's Boxing Gym in West End in his debut professional fight. And Billy Stephen from Boxing'n'Fitness Gym in Ipswich. Both fighters are in the 150-pounds division.'

As our fight began, the crowd got louder. Billy was very good. For the first two rounds we were evenly matched, dancing around each other trying to find vulnerabilities. By the second round my nerves had steadied, but the noise of the cheers and jeers took away my focus, and in the third round, he knocked me to the ground with a punch that left a cut above my eye.

While I staggered to my feet, Billy was closing in ready to attack. The bell rang time before he could land another punch. In the corner, Lucy dabbed my eye with ice-cold cotton wool and then rubbed on petroleum jelly, telling me to keep my focus, and be ready to hit hard when he dropped his guard.

'Stick to the plan, Isa, stick to the plan,' she said.

The fourth round began and I started slow. I threw a couple of punches that missed.

Sun past point midpoint.
I am walking down the track.
1400 hours.

I heard my brother's voice.

> *'Stand up straight! Bend your knees a little bit; your*
> *back straight, head up, your left hand here, your right*
> *hand here. Now, focus, Isa, and follow me. Jab, jab,*
> *duck. You gotta kill this kid.'*
> *'No, I don't want to kill him.'*
> *'Don't be a coward.'*
> *'I'm not a coward.'*
> *'Kill him, then … go, kill him. Jab, jab, duck!'*

The memory threw me off momentarily, but I brought myself back. I got more aggressive and determined. I threw a couple of jabs that propelled Billy off his feet and then I knocked him out with the one-two-three-two combo.

He fell to the ground and didn't move. The crowd went quiet at the thud of his body hitting the mat. Only Tim, Richard and my workmates were cheering and clapping. Their voices were loud.

The referee started counting. Billy was out cold. Not moving. The referee waved his hands, signalling the end of the fight. He raised my hand up while Tim and Lucy rushed inside the ring to celebrate. Tim grabbed me for a hug, dancing round and round with me. The guys from the construction site wanted to buy me a drink.

'You did good,' Lucy said. 'You continue like that, you'll go far.'

I was overwhelmed with joy in my heart. My hard work and the lessons my brother passed on to me had paid off. Regardless of the bruises on my face, I had my first recognised win. After Thommo and the guys rushed me, lifting me up and cheering me more, Lucy called me aside. The boys went to the bar.

She started counting out money. 'You're looking at just under a thousand bucks after training expenses,' she said.

'Is that all?'

'What did you expect? You're at the bottom of the rankings. But not for much longer, I promise. After tonight, I reckon you can win the Australian title. The Asian Pacific, the Southern Hemisphere. I can see you fighting at a big venue like Suncorp Stadium in front of fifty thousand people. I don't just see you becoming the world champion –

I can see you becoming a legend. You'll have anything you want. Money, cars, fame. But you have to have self-control if you're ever gonna become a great fighter.'

I didn't want cars or fame. I just wanted enough money to find Moïse. But now I knew I had a way to do that.

chapter 16

shadow boxing

MY DAYS AND NIGHTS FELL INTO A RHYTHM. I WAS AT
the gym every other evening after my shift and my English
classes. Sometimes we would go to the swimming pool
down the road, sometimes we would just train inside. I
spent a lot of time in the ring sparring with Richard. Feet
stomping on the mats. We pushed hard, until the sweat
made my skin slick.

All the time Lucy was there, watching, correcting and
sharing her thoughts and tips. 'You cannot beat your opponents
unless you know your game. Once you master your game,
then you'll be capable of manipulating your opponent and
changing their game completely so it becomes your own. I'm
going to teach you movement adaptation. When a frog is
placed into cold water, and that water is then placed on a fire
that warms slowly to boiling point, the frog adjusts itself to

the temperature. Unless rescued, it will die because it doesn't resist. So, you need to adapt but not surrender.'

Tim laid out the combos we should work on.

'Watching your last fight, you didn't know what to do in closed spaces,' he said. 'Every time Billy came in closer, you'd panic. Sometimes you didn't have room to set up a whole combination. If you've got an overly aggressive opponent who's invading your space, then you don't have time to start with the jab. Always set up for your right and then follow up with a left hook and another big right hand. When he's open, start with the hard punches right away. This combination is two-three-two: right cross-left hook-right cross. It's good in close range.'

'Get him going in close,' Lucy said as she walked away from the ring. I glanced over to her a few times and saw her speaking animatedly with Richard. A glove to the head brought my attention back to the ring.

Later, Lucy called me into her office.

'Here's a contract for you. I should have talked this through before your fight. It's pretty standard but you might want to show it to someone else before you sign it. Just so you know that I'm not ripping you off. Someone in your family.'

'I don't have a family.'

'Oh, I'm sorry about that. What about a friend, then? Is there anyone you trust who can go through it? Find someone. I don't want any bullshit later on. You can bring it back when you're ready.'

⌐

Two days later, I was at the MDA office showing the contact to Ms Li.

'Are you sure you want to sign this?' she said. 'It ties you up for two years with Clarke's Gym, and Lucy Clarke gets ten per cent of everything you earn. You also have to pay a training fee and equipment levy.'

'Yes, I want to sign.'

'Well, there's nothing bad in here, so it looks okay to me. I'm happy that everything is working out for you, Isa. Good luck with it.' She offered me her hand.

As I walked out I saw Trinity sitting at her desk. She looked at me, smiled and waved.

Walking out the doors of the building I felt someone rush up behind me.

'Hey, you need a lift?' It was Trinity.

'That would be great.'

'I hope you don't mind a small detour?'

As we drove, Trinity told me we were going to pick up her son, Ben, from childcare.

'I didn't know you had a child.'

'His father left me when I told him I was pregnant. He didn't want anything to do with me. I grew up in a Christian family, and my father freaked when I told him and Mum. He told me I was a disgrace to the family. I had to drop out of uni to have Ben, but then Mum started helping me while I finished my degree. And she looks after him a couple of days a week and he goes to childcare the other three. My father still won't look at me properly but at least he speaks to me now. He loves Ben.'

I didn't know what to say, so I just listened.

I waited in the car while Trinity went into the centre, and when she came out she introduced me to Ben. He had the biggest smile on his face and was not bothered meeting a stranger.

'He's always happy and always wants to play,' Trinity said.

'I'm hungry,' Ben said.

'And he's always hungry,' said Trinity, laughing.

We went to McDonald's and sat next to the playground while Ben ate his Happy Meal. He told me about a puppy he wanted to get. Trinity shook her head, so to distract Ben I started playing on the equipment with him.

Back in the car, Ben started to doze off and Trinity asked me about my family. I didn't want to tell her about the horror, so just said I came to Australia alone and that my family were back in the DRC. That was sort of true.

As Trinity pulled up outside the gym she noticed a poster on a telegraph pole advertising my upcoming fight at Mansfield Tavern. I was going to fight Samuel Okwui, a Nigerian fighter living in Toombul.

'Is that you? Impressive!' She flashed another of her smiles as I got out of the car and she drove off, with a sleeping Ben in the back. I walked up to the poster and stared at the picture of Samuel. I had to beat him, I had to win that money. I had to find Moïse.

↩

FIGHT NIGHT.

There were a few more Africans in the crowd, and more of my workmates came along again. Even the foreman was there. Among the spectators, I saw Trinity with her friends at the back of the room. The energy in the place fed my adrenalin and this time I had no nerves. I knew what I had to do, and I was going to do it.

The cheers when Samuel Okwui was introduced were loud but they were even louder when the announcer said my name. It felt good.

The first round was a blur and at no time did Samuel stand a chance. I was doing everything right, and he was like a frog in a slow-boiling pot of water. The second round had barely begun when the fight ended with a knockout. I won with a combination of powerful body punches and uppercuts.

In the change room later, Tim told me Lucy was trying to get me a sponsor.

'If he decides to come on board, it means he would cover all your training expenses, food, accommodation, gear, gloves, shorts, protein drinks, gym time. You name it, he'll pay for it.'

'Why?'

'Because he thinks he's gonna make a lot of money out of you.'

While Tim and I were talking, Lucy walked in with the prospective sponsor.

'Isa, I want you to meet Vince Romano,' Lucy said.

'AKA the bunny with the money,' Vince added as he grabbed my hand and pumped it hard. 'That was a hell of a show you put on tonight, boy. Lucy said you were a killer, and she was right. I'm impressed. Now all you have to do is work hard, listen to Lucy and box.'

'Thank you, sir. I'll try.'

'I don't want you to try, I want you to do it.'

'Yes, sir.'

'I like this kid, Lucy. But we gotta give him a professional name. Eezah is too African. What should we call him? What about Steve, huh?'

'Steve?' Tim said, not sounding very impressed. Lucy didn't say a word.

'Yeah, why not? It suits him. Steve "The Killer" Alakia.'

'Alaki,' Tim said.

'That's it! You like that?'

I didn't like the name but I was not going to admit it in front of this man and risk what he was offering and what I needed.

'Yeah, sure.'

'Good boy. You'll go right to the top, kid. I'm off to take the missus to dinner but I'll see you soon.' He blew out of the change room as quickly as he'd blown in, and the smell of his aftershave lingered far longer than he had.

'Mr Romano was a good friend of Des,' said Lucy, 'and he's been a good friend to me over the years. He'll put the money up for a year but expects to earn it back quick, so he wants you to give up your job at the construction site so you can focus on training.'

'In other words, *Steve*, he'll own you lock-stock-and-barrel for a year,' Tim said.

'It will be worth it, I promise you,' said Lucy.

'Can I get an advance?'

'No, but you will get a weekly wage, don't you worry about that,' Lucy said. Tim walked out of the change room without saying a word.

I might not have been getting money upfront, but if I could train harder I was another step closer to my brother. That was a good thing.

As we came out of the change room, I was suddenly surrounded by all my friends. Those from the construction site and some of the guys and girls from the gym. Everyone was making a big fuss of me, high-fiving and wanting to buy me a drink. Julia, one of the kickboxers, leaned on my shoulder as I walked into the bar area with Richard and the rest of the boys, taking selfies.

I looked around for Trinity, and caught her eye. She came over with her friends. 'Congratulations,' she said. 'You looked pretty good up there.'

After a drink, Trinity said she had to pick up Ben from her parents' house, so I said I'd come with her. I said goodbye to everyone and got my payout from Lucy.

I told Trinity about the sponsorship and then waited in the car while she went in to get Ben.

I saw the front door open again a few seconds later and looked up to see a man who must have been her father peering out at the car. He was in a nightrobe and once he realised that there was a man in Trinity's car he started yelling. I wasn't sure if he was yelling at me or calling for Trinity, but eventually Trinity came out with Ben. She was carrying him and stepped around her father. I got out to open the door and heard the front door of the house slam shut. I looked up and her father was gone.

Ben hardly woke as Trinity strapped him into the car seat, and on the drive to my house we barely said a word. As I got out, Trinity apologised about her father. I told her not to worry, but my mind wasn't in the car. It was somewhere else.

THE PEOPLE NEXT door were having another party and the loud music drowned out Trinity's shouted goodbye. I opened the front door and flicked the light switch on. As soon as I put my sports bag down, my phone beeped. It was a picture of Julia and me after the fight. I deleted the photo, then put my winnings in my shoebox. I was edging closer to being able to pay the private investigator. But thinking of that turned my mind towards the DRC. The sound of the loud music was like exploding bombs in my ears. Every bit of it was excruciating. I closed my eyes and had the sensation that bullets were flying above my apartment. I wanted the music to stop; I tried to cover my ears but the music was too loud to block out. The bass sounded like drum beats from another time. I was being drawn into the music. I was being taken into a different world.

Sun past point midpoint.
I am walking down the track.
1400 hours.
Some boy soldiers stand with drums between their legs.
A pile of six, small dead bodies lie in front of me.

Moïse brings another child and drops him on top of the pile. His hands are loose. His legs are hanging and blood is spilling onto the earth.

Kadogo passes me a gallon of kerosene and I pour it on the pile.

Kadogo holds up a stick of flames and hands it to me. I touch it to the liquid and the pile ignites.

The drums stop and the flames rise higher. The shadows on the ground get taller. The smell turns my stomach.

The music stopped suddenly. Out the window a red light strobed. *Light tracer fire.* I started to shake. My bladder felt full and I had the urge to scream. To hit something. To run. I stumbled over the shoebox and landed on the wall. I raised my fist and slammed it into the plaster, over and over, not realising what I was doing until my whole arm pushed through. I pulled back and looked at the blood running down my fingers.

All of a sudden, I heard someone hitting my door. It sounded like a rapid fire of gunshots building to a crescendo. I stumbled towards the noise, wrenched open the door and without thinking or looking lashed out at the dark figures standing there. I didn't know why the police were at my door but as one of them went to grab me I pushed him hard and ran back to my room. I dived under my bed and tried to hide but their boots entered the room and I felt their hands grab at me and drag me out. Handcuffed, two officers walked me to a police car and forced me into the back seat. The partygoers from next door stood around, watching quietly. The music had stopped.

For almost three hours, I was kept in a small room with nothing in it but a small table, on which I rested my hands, still cuffed. Only the sound of the clock on the wall was audible. An officer walked in and said, 'Do you have anyone you can call to be present before we start? A lawyer or a friend?'

I didn't respond. The officer left the room. I listened to the clock tick over the seconds and counted them.

Much later, I heard Lucy's voice outside the room and the door opened.

'You're bloody lucky Vince knows people. As it is, you're gonna have to pay for all the damage you did.' She sighed. 'You put everything at risk tonight, Isa. Do it again, and we're finished.'

She didn't ask me what happened. I wouldn't have known what to say if she did. I didn't know what happened.

Lucy drove me to the apartment to pick up my stuff before driving to the gym. She pulled into the car park and Tim came out of one of the doors of the building behind the gym. He was in his pyjamas and he didn't look happy. He took my things from the boot and we went up the stairs to the first floor of the complex. I hadn't been up there before.

Tim ushered me inside a very basic room with a narrow bed against the wall. The room had a small television set against the brick wall and a bar fridge by the door.

'It's not much but there's everything you need here,' Tim said. 'You'll be sharing the toilet with the other boys. Stinks worse than a stagnant creek in there, but you should be fine,' he said. 'I'll leave you to it and we can talk tomorrow.'

I opened the window above the bed to let some air in. I still didn't know what had happened, or why the police had been there. I lay down and waited for sleep to save me. When it did, the nightmares came.

⌒

THE ROOM WAS hot when I woke, and I got up to find a note under the door. Lucy had arranged with the landlord to fix the wall so he didn't press charges but I still had to move out. The police had agreed not to charge me too. They'd been called to shut down the party and had been knocking on my door to check I was okay because they'd had numerous complaints and I was the closet neighbour. Lucy told them I'd been asleep and hadn't seen that they were cops. It was dark and I'd thought they were rampaging partygoers. The note said I had to cough up $3000 for the landlord and it would all be sweet. But not sweet with her.

I was back to square one. I had already quit my job at the construction site and I'd just lost more than half of my savings. The only hope I had was to get another fight. I had to get back into training.

⌒

THE SUN WAS high up in the sky. High-intensity circuit training was in progress in the shady outdoor ring. Tim had a stopwatch and barked out commands. I was drenched with sweat but I did everything he told me without stopping. Shadow boxing in the open air. Chin-ups on the pole close to where the rusty punching bag was hung. Hitting the massive tractor tyre with a hammer and then lifting it and turning it over and over and over. Running up and down the external stairs. Just when I thought I was done, Tim called for me to do it all over again. My heart beat in my chest like a drum. My stomach was crumbling and my head was spinning.

Finally Tim told me to stop. I went straight to my room and flopped down on my bed. Everything hurt. But the pain meant I was getting closer to Moïse. I called the private investigator.

'Where is the money?' he said.

I asked him if I could send some now and the rest later. I held my breath and couldn't help smiling when he said, 'Okay, but send me a photo of your brother.' I didn't have one. Everything we'd ever owned, every photo ever taken, was long gone. Hearing that, the private investigator sighed down the phone and told me I was making it tough, but he would do his best.

I hung up feeling better than I had in a long time. I tried to call Auntie and the phone rang out again. Putting down the phone, I picked up Moïse's slingshot from under my pillow. *Where are you, Moïse? Where are you?*

chapter 17

you can't be serious

A KNOCK AT THE DOOR WOKE ME. I WAS STILL HOLDING the slingshot as I stumbled in the dark to answer the knock.

'Steve, are you awake?'

I recognised the voice. Julia, the kickboxer. She had been training near me over the past few days. Since the last fight at the Mansfield Tavern she'd sent me messages, but I never replied.

I flicked the light on and opened the door. Julia pushed her way in.

'You been watching porn?'

'Na, na … no.'

She smirked at me and winked. 'We're all going to a karaoke night. You wanna come?'

I didn't want to go and said so.

'That's all right,' Julia said. 'I'll stay in too.' She jumped on my bed and stretched out. 'We can stay right here.'

I didn't understand what she was up to until she stood up and moved closer to me. She put her hand behind my head and moved her lips towards mine. She started to kiss me and I kissed her back, hard. I pushed the door shut and she started to take off my T-shirt. I lifted her up and put her on the bed and lay on top of her. We kissed more and I went to take her shirt off and ripped two buttons as I pulled at the material. I grabbed her breast. I went to kiss her again and pushed her further back, bumping her head. I pushed my body down between her legs. Suddenly, she stopped, frozen. I sensed a change and sat back.

'Why do you have to be so rough?' Her face was angry and she stood up, pulling her shirt together. 'That is not cool, Steve.'

I watched her disappear out the door, and then I lay back on my bed. My heart was beating faster than when I was training. My hands were shaking and my stomach felt sick. I didn't know what had happened, but I knew that what I had done was wrong and it scared me.

I went back down into the gym, hoping I would see Julia so I could say sorry but she was gone. I found Lucy and

Tim in the lounge area watching a video of a fight. They were watching the two fighters carefully and talking about the hits, their balance, taking notes. I sat next to Tim and watched too.

'Who is he?' I asked.

'That's Wayne Durain,' Tim said.

'Queensland's heavyweight champion,' Lucy added. 'Won three consecutive national titles.'

'I want to fight him,' I said.

Tim laughed. 'Are you out of your mind?' he said. 'He's the state champion. He's a hundred times better than anyone you've fought so far. And he's been training properly for years. You are so far from ready, and if you lose to him at this stage in your career it's all over red rover.'

'I can beat him,' I said.

'You can't be serious. Maybe one day, yes,' Tim said.

'I am serious,' I said and I told Lucy and Tim that I was going to do it.

⟵

OVER THE NEXT few days I trained hard. The Brisbane heat made it feel like I was moving through a river, and the

211

humidity zapped everyone's energy, but I pushed on. I saw Julia and smiled but she turned away as soon as I caught her eye. I didn't have time to worry, so I pushed her out of my mind. Every chance I had I was in Lucy and Tim's ears talking about challenging Wayne Durain. I needed that prize money to find Moïse, I needed that fight.

After pestering Lucy and Tim, I talked to Vince. Together they told me that the purse would mean I could earn between seven and ten thousand dollars, maybe more. After hearing that, I pushed even harder. Vince loved the idea. Lucy was coming around, but Tim told me I was putting my whole fighting career on the line. Losing to Wayne would mean the end of me and it would be years before I could try again. That meant losing all my sponsors because no one would want to work with me until I was able to rise through the ranks.

One afternoon, after Vince had just left and Lucy and Tim were arguing about me challenging Wayne, Trinity arrived at the gym with her little boy, Ben. She was holding his hand, and she waved over to me and then to Richard and Lee who had paused their sparring to see who the kid was. Ben was very excited to see me. He wriggled his arm to escape Trinity's hand and ran to me for a hug. He was holding a little orange envelope. Trinity chased Ben, smiling apologetically. Everybody else went back to what they were doing and Lucy and Tim went into the office.

'Sorry to bother you, but Ben was worried he wouldn't see you,' Trinity said. 'He wanted to invite you to his birthday party.'

Ben reached up to hand me the envelope. 'I'm five. You come to my party?'

I opened the letter to see a brightly coloured handmade card. 'I would like very much to come,' I told him.

He started watching Richard and Lee and was wide-eyed as they hit out at each other's gloves. He wanted to jump into the ring, so I found the smallest pair of gloves we had, which were still far too large, and showed him how to move his hands and his feet. Jab-jab-duck. He started to mimic my moves. Jab-jab-duck. Trinity was laughing, and I pretended that Ben had knocked me over. It felt good to be with them both, and hearing Ben's giggles and seeing the smile on his face gave me joy. When I said goodbye I felt happier than I had in a long time.

That evening Lucy told me that she'd set up a meeting with Wayne Durain's coach. I was going to get the fight.

The next night Lucy, Tim, Vince and I met with Wayne's coach, Jimmy, over dinner at Mansfield Tavern. We'd barely sat down and Vince was talking fast about the business of the fight. I sat quietly, not saying much until I heard Jimmy say, 'We are not fighting this monkey. He needs to go back into the jungle and eat some bananas. Not in the ring with my fighter. Not on my watch.'

'Who are you calling monkey, you arsehole?' Tim said as he stood up to leave. I wanted to reach across the table and deck Jimmy but I needed this fight. Lucy placed her hand on Tim's arm to restrain him and said, 'We'll give you eighty per cent of the door whether you win or not. Think about it.'

Jimmy glared at Tim and shoved his chair from the table. Then he walked away.

'Why did you say that?' Tim asked.

'Because we're gonna beat that bastard, and when we do, it will put us in the number-one contender spot for the national title. That's why,' Lucy said.

That's exactly what I wanted to hear.

chapter 18

ghosts

FOR THE NEXT FEW WEEKS, I PREPARED MYSELF TO FIGHT the number-one contender and steal his belt. I knew I had to work extremely hard, harder than ever before, if I was to win against the three-time national champion. My reflexes had to be much sharper and my speed had to improve. Vince spoke to Lucy and Tim and said he'd pay for an intensive camp so we could really step things up, so we all went down to the Gold Coast to train at one of Vince's playgrounds. Lucy, Tim and I went in Lucy's Merc while Richard, Lee, Johnny and one other new fighter, Tony, drove down in a different vehicle.

We arrived at a big, gated double-storey mansion that had a couple of dolphin statues on either side of the entrance with streams of water flowing down from their mouths. A few cars were parked outside the garage.

Vince gave us a tour of his multi-million-dollar house. It had a tennis court and basketball court. On the other side of the house was a boxing ring next to an Olympic-size swimming pool. The ground floor of the house had a huge statue of a lion right in the centre of the main entrance foyer. The house also had a ten-seat theatre, a conference room, a jacuzzi and a gambling area. I had never seen anything like it – it was like a king's palace. I trailed behind Vince wondering how much money you would have to have to afford a home like this. Vince was talking about the training schedule and I was listening carefully until, at the back of the house, in the shade near the veranda, I saw a couple of animal skins hanging from the rafters. The smell of smoke drifted over from a fire that someone had lit in a pizza oven and the smell and the skins took my mind back.

'Those are 'roo skins, Steve,' Vince said. 'Ever eaten a kangaroo? We sell them in some of my restaurants. Best meat in the world. No fat. You should try it sometime.' His words jumbled together and I stopped listening. My eyes were fixed on those skins. My mind seemed to jump and I was suddenly a long way from that Gold Coast mansion …

Sun past point midpoint.

I am walking down the track.

1400 hours.

One at a time we went in and out of the small hut.

Animal skins were hanging from the rafters.

Bones were wrapped around the witch-doctor's ankles, elbows and neck.

I chewed down hard on the small stick the witch-doctor had given me.

I felt a burning and a sting as I looked up at the sharp blade of a machete ...

'Steve! Steve! Mate, earth to Steve,' Vince shouted.

I shook my head of memories and followed Vince to the back of the house where a covered pergola was filled with high-end professional gym equipment. More than what we had at the gym.

The boxing ring beside the equipment looked like it had just been built; everything was shiny and new. Tim gave a whistle as he walked over and told me we would start out in the pool. Most of the time I wasn't doing laps, I was running through the water with my hands raised up high. The faster I got to the other side, the better. The other guys got in too and we competed to see who was the fastest.

After the pool work I got into the ring with Tim. I followed his moves, his hands forming a fist, and watched his shoulders moving and his legs wobbling as his head shook from side to side.

'I'm coming at you, I'm coming at you but you don't know what I'm going to throw at you and you'll never know what I'm going to do. One-two. One-two-three. One-two-six-three. One-two-slip. You don't know when I'm coming. You don't know what I'm throwing. You don't know which way I'm coming in, you don't know which way I'll go out,' Tim said. He pushed me until my own legs were wobbling from exhaustion and the lactic acid build-up burned.

At the end of our session, we all sat in Vince's theatre watching tapes of Wayne Durain's fights, studying all his moves and all his mistakes.

'You're gonna know every move he's ever made by heart by the time of the fight,' Lucy said.

I was excited and nervous at the same time. I had never dreamed of coming this far.

We spent two weeks at Vince's, training, planning,

and in the first week Lucy nailed down a date and time for the fight. The posters were made and by the time we were back in Brisbane I was ready. The waiting was the hard part.

⌐

THE NOISE WAS deafening. I walked into Mansfield Tavern and it was packed tight with spectators. Everyone was cheering and clapping. The atmosphere was exuberant. I looked around and finally found Trinity's face in the crowd. Thommo and the construction crew were there, and so were Ryan and Lachlan from the PCYC. Vince was right up the front near the judges' table. But there were many more faces I didn't know, and the sound of the crowd made me nervous. Lucy and Tim grabbed me and walked me into the change room before I could say hello to anyone. I got into my gear and Lucy put my gloves on. Tim told me calmly that I knew what I had to do – now I just had to do it. I tried to block out the noise as we walked back out. A well-dressed man in black pants and a crisp white shirt with a bow tie stepped into the centre of the ring.

'Ladies and gentlemen. Welcome to our main event for this evening. Ten rounds to decide the number-one contender for the Australian heavyweight title. Our referee for this contest is Mr Nick Lorenzo. Firstly, introducing the blue corner, trained by Lucy Clarke, from Clarke's Gym in West End, Brisbane: official weight, 85.5 kilograms, standing five feet eleven inches, tonight wearing the green shorts with a white trim, still undefeated, fifteen fights, fifteen wins, nine by way of knockout – he is the beast with the fist of iron, ladies and gentlemen. The rising star, fighting to become the number-one contender for Australia's heavyweight champion. All the way from the Congo, via Brisbane, please make him welcome: Steve "The Killer" Alaki!'

The crowd applauded as I walked in jumping up and down to the Congolese music. My team of Lucy, Tim and the rest of the guys from the gym were behind me.

'And now, to my left, introducing the red corner, the former three-time national champion and the current state champion, trained by Jimmy Fisher from Fisher's Gym in Victoria Point, Western Brisbane: official weight, 85.8 kilograms, standing six feet, tonight wearing the black shorts with a white trim. He has defended his title five times. With a professional fight record of thirty-two fights, twenty-six wins, twelve by way of knockout: Wayne "The Pain" Durain!'

The crowd went nuts as Wayne walked into the ring with his title belt around his shoulder. The referee called us to the middle to give us instructions before starting the fight. 'Protect yourselves at all times, keep your punches above the waist at all times. Have a clean fight. Understand?' We touched gloves and went back to our corners.

'Don't give him any leeway. Make sure he remembers your name, Killer!' Tim said.

'Okay, Isa, you've got this one. He's nothing. Worse than nothing – he's a has-been. He's slow now but you're a killer. Listen to Tim while you're in there, okay? Only Tim. Make me proud!' Lucy said.

The bell rang and the fight was underway. I ducked and weaved, staying out of Wayne's way. I could hear Tim shouting, 'Now jab! Jab! Keep moving! Get out of there!' I wasn't throwing any jabs. I was distracted and overwhelmed. Tim continued shouting at me. 'You're a killer, Isa, you're a killer.' Wayne attacked me and landed a left hook to my head. I staggered on my feet.

Sun past point midpoint.

I am walking down the track.

1400 hours.

I'm creeping through green grass.

Angry birds singing uncontrollably.

One, two, three civilians in my sight.

My gun is loaded and ready for impact.

Two more approaching …

Bones quiver.

My body squats.

Salty flood spilling down my chest.

The sun bursts in the blue sky.

More mass. My heart rusts with dust.

The locals learn to lapidate rebellion.

Burning rocks fly above my head.

'Jab! Jab!' Tim shouted. I threw a combo that slowed Wayne down just before the bell rang for the end of the first round.

'That's how you finish! You started a bit slow but you picked it up! Don't worry about that hit, you just have to keep those jabs going. Remember, you are a killer. Always have been, always will. Now get out there, Isa, it's killing time,' Lucy said as she wiped the sweat off my face.

Her words resembled those of the Messiah I once knew. The same instructions I was given before going to war. *You kill or get killed.* But Lucy had told me this isn't war. That it's a game where you shake hands at the end of it. So I pushed Matete's voice from my thoughts.

I got back in the ring, ready and dangerous. I liked fighting against the odds. Everybody was cheering Wayne's name except for the people I knew. But as the fight went on, more people started calling my name. By the seventh round I was reading his mind. He was getting tired on his feet. I was in charge and on top. Until ... I saw a face in the crowd. Maybe it was a vision, or maybe it was real ...

'What's your name?' I asked.

'Jacob,' the boy replied. He looked younger than me. Maybe he was eight or so.

'You're not Jacob. From now on, you're Delta Force. Come with me.'

I made him kill on his first day of being recruited.

Silent night!

Lift fist!

Sharp blades.

Skin bleeds.

Sweet bleat.

Falling crows.

Let their shadows cover the ground like black sand.

Decomposing corpses filled with louse.

This one still has fresh wounds. Inestimable bruises.

Two more corpses.

My heart crumbles with thunder.

They get closer so, careless! I am fearless!

Dirt boots step on fireworks.

Foot works.

'Isa, are you still in the fight?' Tim shouted. 'You have to finish that bastard!'

Wayne was on his toes. The crowd was getting louder and I was gaining strength. He stumbled on his feet, and I followed up with more body punches that knocked him down.

As he fell to the canvas, I continued punching him until the referee came to separate us. 'The fight's over!' the referee shouted. He checked on my opponent. Blood was dripping down his face and pooling on the canvas. I couldn't look away. The colour of blood is the same no matter what country you are in.

Tim and Lucy rushed into the ring and threw their arms around me. 'You did us proud,' Lucy said.

I looked over her shoulder, searching for Delta Force, but he wasn't there. While Lucy and Tim celebrated, I felt completely removed. As soon as I could I rushed outside, but there was no sign of him. As I turned back I heard somebody call 'Cyborg!' and a figure emerged from the shadows of the building.

I grabbed him by the neck and threw him against the wall, studying his face thoroughly. It all came flooding back. It was him.

'What happened to my brother?' I asked.

'Rambo? I don't know.'

'Tell me what happened to him!' I yelled.

'I swear I don't know.'

I raised my fist, about to punch him. His hands went up to protect his face. Then, I let him go and he dropped to the ground. 'You tell people about me and you're dead. Understand?'

He nodded, and I left him there. I ran back inside to get my stuff and then went to find Trinity.

'Can we get out of here?'

⌒

TRINITY DROVE WHILE I sat in the front seat and said nothing. My mind was no longer present. It was racing and pacing between time zones.

'You looked good out there,' she said.

I was staring out the window, not seeing what was in front of me, only what was behind.

'Are you all right?' Trinity asked. 'You should be happy and proud. You won the state title!'

'I'm just tired. I wanna get home,' I said. I didn't even know where home was anymore.

'Okay.' After a few moments, she added: 'The next time you fight, you should wear the Congolese flag as your uniform. The yellow and blue would look good on you. That's how people could know where you are from.'

I nodded but couldn't find any words. As Trinity pulled up outside the gym I jumped out and said thank you. I shut the door quickly and didn't watch her drive away.

I got into my room, shut the door and locked it like there was a ghost outside. And there was. I stood leaning against the door in the dark. I took out my phone to call the private investigator in Goma, but he wasn't reachable. I didn't try Auntie or Nyota. I knew in my heart they were gone. I let my body slide down the door and I sat in the dark thinking about what had just happened.

I stayed inside my room for two days. I stayed quiet and didn't make a sound and no one knew I was there. I could hear the shouts and cheers from the gym so I knew everyone was still celebrating. They saw me leave the fight with Trinity, so they must have thought I was still with her. But I had shut down, emotionally and physically. On the evening of the second day, just as hunger made me think I might have to leave my room, my phone rang. It was the private investigator.

'I have bad news.'

My stomach started to crumble. My feet started to sweat. I was waiting for the worst news I could possibly get.

'You didn't tell me your brother was a child soldier,' he said.

'What difference does it make?' I asked the man.

'It makes it much harder to track him down. If he is alive, he probably doesn't want to be found. He could be charged with war crimes. A few child soldiers have faced that and if they are charged they could be sentenced to life imprisonment or even death. You should have told me. I wouldn't have taken your money.'

'Well, give it back then,' I said.

'It's too late. I've had expenses.' He paused. 'I'm sorry Isa, I can't take this case any further.'

I didn't know what else to say, so I just said goodbye.

As I hung up I realised how dangerous it would be for Moïse – and for me – if I contacted any authorities to try to find him.

I took my brother's slingshot and went down to the park, where what seemed like a thousand flying foxes were hanging upside down in the large trees.

'*You must have a good eye to kill a bird,*' my brother used to tell me. '*See a bird, aim, and then release.*' I took aim at a bat and fired. They all took off in a rush of noise and wind and screeching, filling the sky with a black cloud. A couple of them dropped down as they struggled to fly in the crowded space. I looked to the ground to find the one I'd hit but there were several dying bats on the ground. My brother would be proud of me. He used to tell me I didn't know how to target. My father would be proud of me too. But they were both gone and I had let them both down. I had watched my mother, my sister and my father die, and then I left my brother behind. I was no longer the child who dreamed of becoming like my father.

I had let my whole family down. Maybe I would never see my brother again.

Maybe I would be better off dead too.

chapter 19

you don't know me

TWO DAYS LATER I WENT TO BEN'S BIRTHDAY PARTY IN the park. Trinity had been there for hours hanging streamers and balloons above the shade poles and making sure she had the perfect table near the barbecue. It was a riot of colour and looked so happy and fun. When I got there, Trinity and her mother, Mrs Maumbe, were cooking little hot dogs, steaks and other party snacks on the barbecue. A crowd of kids, a mix of whites, Asians and Africans, with painted faces and wearing party hats, were running everywhere. As soon as Ben saw me he ran up and wrapped his arms around my legs. A group of kids stood behind him as I gave him his present. He sat down right there and ripped off the paper. A box of Lego. He wanted to play with it there and then but Trinity called out for him to bring it over to the picnic rug so he didn't lose any pieces.

Ben did as his mother told him, and the other kids and I went and sat down, watching and helping.

Everyone was having a great time until Trinity's father, Mr Maumbe, arrived at the park with more guests. Among them was Delta Force. Trinity smiled and rushed over to grab him by the hand and bring him to where I was playing with Ben and the other children.

'What's he doing here?' I asked Trinity.

'I invited him.'

'Why?'

'He said he knew you! And I told him you'd be here,' Trinity's face had moved from excited to puzzled. She didn't know what was wrong but she could tell something was. She made her way back to the barbecue, leaving me and Delta Force standing above the crowd of kids on the picnic rug.

'Can we talk?' he said.

'You stay away from me.' I didn't realise I was yelling until I noticed everyone at the park turn their faces towards us. I started to walk away but Delta Force followed.

'I just want to talk, I need to. Only you can understand,' he said.

'I don't want to talk to you. Now, get away from me.'

I pushed him with such force that he fell backwards to the ground. People started to run over and I kept walking.

'Isa, what's happening?' Trinity ran towards me.

I shouted, 'Leave me alone!'

I had tears running down my face but I didn't know how long I had been crying. I ran across the park. I stopped at a bus stop and tried to settle my mind. My thoughts were jumbled and I felt like my mind was tearing in two. I had a pain in my head and in my heart. Eventually I stood and started running again, all the way back to the gym.

As soon as I arrived, I saw Trinity's car parked behind the building. She saw me and got out of the car, clutching something in her hand.

'You want to tell me what all of that was about back there?' she asked.

'Nothing! It's none of your business,' I said. I saw the flash of hurt cross her face.

'Jacob asked me to give you this envelope.' Trinity shoved it in my hand. 'What is going on?' she said, her voice breaking.

'I'm sorry,' I said.

'I'm sorry, too, I thought we were friends.'

'You don't know me! If you did, you wouldn't want to be friends with me or have me anywhere near your son,' I said.

'Why don't you tell me who you are, then? Let *me* decide if I want to be your friend.'

I said nothing.

'Does Jacob know who you are?'

'What did he tell you?' I said.

'He told me you were friends.'

'We are *not* friends.'

Lucy appeared at the top of the stairs and started to climb down.

'Is everything all right here?' she asked.

'Yeah!' I yelled. I turned to Trinity and said, 'Tell Ben I'm sorry for running off and not saying goodbye. I can't talk now.' I started towards the stairs, passing Lucy as I went. Trinity was crying as I walked away, and I heard Lucy say: 'I don't want you upsetting him like that. He's got a big fight coming up. And he's on track to win. I don't want anything or anyone getting in the way of that. You understand?' I didn't hear Trinity's reply.

I went to my room and lay down on my bed, still holding the envelope. I wanted to throw it away, but I couldn't. I had to look. I opened it and found a small memory card. I put it in my phone and opened it up. It had a collection of old pictures of Delta Force's time in the DRC. I went through all the pictures until I came across one of us: Delta Force and me. It was a picture he took after the celebration in the rebel camp. I scrolled down to another picture: Moïse and Delta Force. My brother was still young, maybe seventeen. His face was filled with a guardedness and sorrow, but there was a confidence there that hadn't diminished, despite the horrors we had seen. I zoomed in to look at the image properly. It was the first time I had seen my brother's face in seven years. I felt tears rolling down my face again. I didn't think I could have many left in my eyes that day.

There was a soft knock on the door. I opened it, and Trinity was there. I stepped into her hug and cried. She held me until the sobs stopped. That took a long time. I stepped back and she shut the door and sat down on my bed.

'This is my brother,' I said, holding up the photo of him. 'That's Moïse. He taught me how to box.'

'Is that why you like fighting? Because of him?' she said.

'When I fight, I hear him speaking to me,' I said. 'I hear his voice, when I'm in the ring. It brings me closer to him.'

'What happened to him?' she asked.

'I don't know. I don't know if he is alive or dead. I've tried to find him but I haven't been able to get anywhere,' I said.

'Someone must know,' Trinity said. 'I can only imagine what happened to you both. You don't have to tell me, but I can talk to people at work and help you through my network. And don't worry, I won't say too much. Just what they'll need to know.'

Trinity typed her email address into my phone and I heard it ping as the photo of Moïse sent. Trinity left to get back to Ben but as she was closing the door to my room she paused and said, 'I know who you are, Isa Alaki, and you are my friend.'

chapter 20

silent night

THE WEEKS AFTER BEN'S PARTY WENT QUICKLY, AND Trinity kept me updated on what she was doing to try to find Moïse. I was concentrating on my next fight and trying not to hope too hard that I would soon hear news of my brother.

Lucy knew something was going on and came up to me after a training session. 'Listen here, Stevie. Forget about all the other fights you've won. The next one is what we've been fighting for. If you win this fight, you'll be a champion. You hear that, Stevie? The Australian Heavyweight Champion. I have faith in you! From the very moment I saw you, I knew you'd be a champion.'

My next fight was to be against the Australian Heavyweight champion Jeff Wilkie. With a couple of championship belts to his name, Lucy was right, he was my biggest challenge so far.

Vince and the promoter had organised a press conference to announce the championship fight. Lucy, Tim and I, along with other members of the gym, arrived at the Sofitel Hotel, where the media conference was to take place. It was a fancy hotel but not as fancy as Vince's place on the Gold Coast. I don't think any place would ever match that. We were welcomed by camera flashes and had to negotiate a path around boom mics. A long table was set at the front of the hall where I sat alongside Lucy, Tim and Vince. Jeff Wilkie and his team sat at the other end of the table, with the promoter between our teams. There was a crowd of about fifty people from various media. Everything was new to me. I was feeling nervous about being in the spotlight, while Jeff sat there looking comfortable.

The promoter made all the necessary introductions, then continued. 'We're going to start with questions. One at a time. Make it clear to whom the question is being addressed.'

A tall man raised his hand and said, 'My question is to Steve. Do you think you can beat Wilkie?'

'I think so,' I said.

The same journalist then asked: 'Any danger it might be too soon? You've had less than twenty professional fights compared to Jeff Wilkie, who has defended his title against more experienced fighters. Wouldn't you like to win a few more fights before you face an experienced boxer like Wilkie?'

'I think now is the right time.'

A question came from the other side of the room. 'My question is to Jeff Wilkie. How does it feel to you, a champion, to be fighting someone nobody's ever heard of?'

Lucy spoke quickly, 'After this fight everyone in Australia will know who Steve Alaki is.'

'Excuse me, Ms Clarke, the question was addressed to Mr Wilkie,' the Promoter said. 'Please, Jeff, go ahead.'

'Everyone wants a shot at the champ, their punishment will happen in the ring,' he said.

Questions kept flying from around the room.

'My question is to Steve. Whereabouts in the Congo are you from?'

'Bukavu, near the eastern border.'

'Is that where all the fighting is? Did you fight?'

Lucy jumped in before I could reply. 'Steve left Africa when he was really young. He was deemed a refugee before coming to Australia. End of story.'

The camera flashes were blinding. I thought of the day my father stood in front of cameras giving his speech on freedom and liberation.

Australia had given me freedom, and after that day it seemed I was suddenly one of their own. I was everywhere – on the television news, in magazines and newspapers. 'Young Congolese refugee taking the boxing world by storm,' the headlines read.

The crew at the gym kept me focused. Whenever something came on the TV about me we would all stop what we were doing and watch and they'd make fun of how I looked or of how funny my English sounded on television. It was good-natured, not cruel, and it made me laugh.

The media attention kept building. Most days TV cameras would be at the gym to document my training and I was wanted on every television talk-show. Radio stations wanted to interview me. Lucy and Tim managed it all and made sure nothing got in the way of my training schedule. But I still found time to hang out with Trinity and Ben at the park, or the swimming pool at South Bank. I was a minor celebrity. It felt good signing autographs. Then, one day, another TV crew came to the gym to film me sparring. After I was done, the reporter took his phone out and showed me a clip.

'One more thing, Steve. I'd like you to have a look at this and give me your response.'

The reporter played a video of me with the caption 'Killer Alaki'. It was grainy mobile phone footage of the altercation in the Valley – it showed me knocking the drunk guy with the guitar to the ground. At first it was hard to tell who the figure was, but my face was clearly visible when I ran past the camera.

'Is that you, Steve?' he asked. 'It *is* you, isn't it?'

'What is that?' I said.

'You don't know?' he responded. 'Are you denying it's you?' he said.

'No, it's me! I was just trying to help out that woman,' I said.

'Which woman?' he asked.

The video didn't show more than me swinging the guitar at the drunk guy as he fell down, and then running off.

The reporter then said, 'There's something else.' He played me film of my ex-landlord cleaning up the wreckage of my old apartment.

'What about this, then?' he said. 'Recognise him? This man was your landlord. And you trashed his apartment, leaving holes in the walls.'

The reporter's voice had hardened, and his cameraman was still filming. Lucy raced over and stood between me and the reporter. 'Okay, that's enough. Turn the cameras off. Now!' she shouted. 'You came here to film training, not to throw our session into chaos with your questions. I want you all to leave. Fuck off!'

While the TV crew were packing up, Lucy called me into her office, shutting the door behind us and winding down the blinds.

'That wasn't good, Steve. Is there anything else I should know about you? Anything else likely to make an appearance on the Internet?'

I didn't know what else to do. I just shook my head.

⌣

Two DAYS PASSED, and things seemed to settle down. But one of the evening news shows had advertised a story about me. All we could do was wait.

241

When it aired, it was bad. It started with the footage of Lucy losing it at the reporter who came to film our training session and then played the grainy footage of me and the drunk guy. The reporter backgrounded it with reports of me vandalising my apartment and then said, 'I am not alleging Steve Alaki has committed war crimes, but he does come from a notorious war zone. It certainly raises questions about who we let into our country and how much we know about what they did before they came here.'

The host then introduced a discussion panel on violence in sport and in the community. They played footage of war – houses being set on fire and a frame showing people lying on the ground, mostly half-burnt. Everyone in the gym turned to look at me, and I could see the horror on Lucy's face. I wanted to say something but my mind went black. The memories I had locked away broke out and overwhelmed me and I couldn't get them out of my mind's eye.

Sun past point midpoint.
I am walking down the track.
1400 hours.
I'm creeping through green grass.

*I hear explosions. I hear screaming children as I,
along with the other boy soldiers, run from one house
into the next on the signal of our leader barking orders.
We loot, and shoot at anything that moves. Throw
hand grenades and use our machetes to kill those people
we capture. Kadogo shouts orders at me and I run into
a small house, breaking down the door with my AK-
47. The place is deserted. Half-burnt furniture, roof
smoking and holes through which I can see the sky. No
sign of life here. Through the backdoor window, I see
two men in government army uniforms with their guns
aimed at me as they approach the house slowly.*

*Without hesitation, I open fire. Both men go down,
white hot metal piercing their chests. My mind is
frozen. It's getting colder. Kadogo bursts into the house.
Out the window he sees the government uniforms lying
on the ground.*

'You're just like me.'

'Isa … Isa … ISA!' Lucy and Tim shouted. 'Are you okay?'

I didn't respond; instead I ran straight to my room.
Everything I had ever seen was flowing back to me. For a
while every night had been a living memory. Every sleep

a trip to a horror film. But I thought I had finally left it behind. Now, it was all back. A waking nightmare with no end. I was being taken back to the life I once lived. But, this time, I was re-living it from my room in the day, not in my sleep. My nightmares were taking a piece of me. They were stealing my mind and my future.

The next day I tried to shake it off. Went back to my training routine. But everything was different. Richard and I sweated it out, sparring under the heavy sun, and Tim and Lucy stood on the sidelines coaching as usual. But my mind wasn't in the right place. I was swinging jabs from side to side, and I was all over the shop. In a game of advantages, Richard threw a jab that went straight to my face. I pushed him over and we ended up on the ropes squaring up at each other until Tim separated us.

Lucy rushed over to me. 'What the hell are you doing?' she said. 'Focus! The fight is in your head. Learn to control it. You're a professional boxer not a street fighter. We've got the biggest fight of our lives in five days. Win the next fight and the sky is the limit. It's up to you, Steve.' She walked away and went back inside the gym.

'What's going on?' Tim asked. 'You have to stay focused. You can win. Just take a break.'

I backed away with my hands up in the air. 'Sorry, Richard,' I said.

'All good in the hood, mate,' Richard responded.

I went to my room and found fifteen missed calls from Trinity. I called her back.

'Hey, Isa. I have news. The Red Cross want to give Moïse's photo to Interpol.'

'Interpol? Who's that?'

'International Police.'

'No police, Trinity.'

'But they're really good at finding missing persons. They can do a projection to see what Moïse would look like now.'

'No police.'

'Isa, you have to trust someone.'

I wanted to find Moïse and I couldn't do it alone. Maybe Trinity was right. We spoke some more and she talked me into meeting with her legal-aid colleague, to assure me that it would be all right to involve the police.

Trinity also convinced me to meet with Delta Force, in case he knew something that could help. She said she would come after work to pick me up. After I hung up the phone I felt a little more together. I was doing something, and that was better than waiting for the nightmares to come.

⌐

I WAS ON the street as Trinity pulled up. The sun was just setting and I watched a cloud of bats fly through the sky. The heat of the day bounced back off the road and as I opened the door the cool of the air-conditioned car was like a wake-up call. I sat next to Trinity as she drove to Moorooka, and I started to tell her what had happened to me. To Delta Force, and about Matete and Kadogo. I trusted her.

Eventually she asked me, 'What are you going to say to Jacob?'

'I want to tell him that I'm sorry. I want him to forgive me.'

'What would you do if you came face to face with Matete? Would you forgive him?'

'Never. But I would want to hear him admit that what he did was wrong.'

It was dark when we drove into the community housing area. We saw a lot of flashlights. There were ambulances and three police vehicles parked outside the building. The place was in an uproar, with cops everywhere, and we had no idea what was going on. Congolese people were milling around on the lawn outside, weeping and shouting. The police stopped our car and told us we could go no further. Trinity parked and we got out and walked to the address she had for Delta Force. She told me to call him by his real name, Jacob.

As we got closer, two paramedics walked out with a body on a stretcher. A hospital blanket covered it and it was strapped down. They don't cover the head if a person is alive. I stood and watched as Trinity went over to one of the women she knew who was wandering aimlessly. They talked briefly before Trinity came back to me. She put her arms around me. She didn't say a word as she started sobbing.

Silent night.

I knew.

I broke away from Trinity and started to run out into the busy four-lane road. I ducked and weaved through traffic to get to the other side. Cars were honking and braking, and somehow I made it without getting hit. Once I got across the road, I kept running.

I ran from Moorooka to the Story Bridge. My feet were pounding the cement of the bridge's footpath. I stopped halfway and climbed up on the railing on the side of the bridge. Cars sped by me but I heard nothing as I stared down into the inky-dark Brisbane River. The water was deep, and a long way down.

chapter 21

remembering

Sun past point midpoint.

I am walking down the track.

1400 hours.

I see it all. I see it now. Half-burnt furniture around me. I smell cooked flesh. It's too silent in here. I check in all the rooms but find nothing. Before I take off, I hear a small voice coming from one of the bedrooms. Someone coughing. I go back inside and find a small boy hiding under the bed. Terrified. His hands on his head.

'You're coming with me,' I say.

The boy starts crying and shaking at the same time.

'What's your name?' I ask.

'Jacob,' the boy replies.

He looks much younger than me. Maybe eight or so.

'*You're not Jacob. From now on, you're Delta Force.
Come with me.*'

*Two army trucks are parked by a large compound,
exploded pieces of grenades and launched rockets are
scattered around the yard.*

*A wounded government soldier half-runs and half-
drags his leg towards the trucks as Delta Force and I
walk into the compound. Soon after, Kadogo appears
with a small group of soldiers, shouting and yelling.
The government soldier grabs his handgun and shoots.
It hits a boy from my school who is walking with
Kadogo. As we all move to attack him, the soldier has
no more bullets left. With his hand on the door of the
truck, he tries to take the car keys from his pocket to
enter but it's too late, one of the boys slices his hand
with a machete. The soldier screams in desperation.
The whole group surrounds him, but he's still holding
onto his hand.*

'*Delta Force!*' *I shout as I give him my machete.*
'*Kill him!*' *Delta Force hesitates. His eyes start to drop
rain. His nose is getting sweaty.* '*Never look your victim
in the eyes before you kill them. Otherwise, they'll stay
with you forever. Kill him, Delta Force, do it now!*'

The government soldier looks up in despair and disbelief. Without looking, Delta Force slices. A head spins on the ground as it disconnects from the soldier's body. Blood floods the tyres like a flowing river. Silent night.

I am here for a demolition.

My mind was frozen. Everything came to me vividly. No escaping doors or windows.

I stood on the bridge a long time, until the sound of a siren getting closer made me move. I had to decide: jump or fight on.

I went back to the gym and hit the punching bag until it split open. My heart was racing faster than ever before. My mind was long gone. Lucy, observing from her office window, came up to me, watching what I was doing.

'What's wrong with you, young man?' she asked.

I started to walk away.

'Don't you walk away from me. You need to get your head right, son. We only have three days till the big fight.'

'I sometimes see things in the ring,' I said without turning to her.

'What things?'

'My parents ... Rita, Moïse, Kadogo ...'

'You have to get that out of your head. I can teach you technique but I can't get inside your brain. You've worked so hard to get to this point. Don't throw all of it away.'

I didn't know if I could stop the memories coming. The banks of the river had broken. Knowing Delta Force was under that blanket had knocked out the locked doors in my mind and it all kept coming back to me. The sounds, the smells, the fear, the dread.

'Just get your mind right, son,' Lucy said as she squeezed my shoulder. I didn't know if I could.

LUCY KEPT ME hungry for the weigh-in until the Friday night. We went down to the Convention Centre, in front of television cameras and spectators. Jeff Wilkie wore his championship belt, taking it off and holding it high before stepping on the scales. The tension was rising and I was ready to battle with my fists and not my AK-47. I tried to shut off the memories and concentrate on that moment.

I was set to accomplish one thing. My fists and my body were ready to get into the rhythm of the fight.

The next night was fight night. The sound of spectators roaring from the main venue was like a wild beast. The energy was heightened. My team were wearing T-shirts with *Team Alaki* printed on the back. In the change room we all stood in a circle, holding hands. We prayed. Hidden under the long silk dressing gown were my blue-and-yellow shorts. Congolese colours.

An official came into the rooms to remind me of the fight rules. 'Great sportsmen show great conduct,' he said. 'Respect each other in the ring and remember to keep your punches above the waist at all times, have a clean fight, have fun and good luck to you.'

When he left, Lucy stepped up and said, 'The greatest battle is won one step at a time, Isa. Remember, you came to me and wanted to be a prize fighter. You've got yourself here. You go out there and make us proud.'

Tim and Richard told me I had this, and then it was time.

A blue boxing ring sat in the middle of the venue with four flat screens hanging above. In the middle of the ring stood the announcer in a silver dinner jacket, surrounded by two girls in bikinis. Another man in a bow tie stood next to him.

The announcer called me first. I walked to the ring and saw more people in the audience than I had ever seen before. Some shouted and clapped as my entourage walked to the ring. The crowd got louder when Jeff Wilkie was introduced.

'Ladies and gentlemen, welcome to our main event here at the Brisbane Convention Centre. Ringside, the three judges scoring the bout are Dennis Parker, Andreas Carlos and James Carlton. Inside the ring, the man in charge of the action is Flynn Taylor. The fighters are in the ring and they are ready. For the thousands in the arena and the millions watching around the world, let's get ready to rumble.

'Twelve rounds to decide the Australian Heavyweight Champion. Firstly, introducing the blue corner. Trained by Lucy Clarke from Clarke's Gym in West End, Brisbane: official weight 87.3 kilograms, standing five feet eleven inches, tonight wearing the blue shorts with yellow trim, still undefeated in his campaign of professional boxing; sixteen fights, thirteen wins, four by way of knockout, he's the people's champion, the newborn all the way from Africa via Brisbane, the challenger, the number-one contender – please make him welcome, Steve "The Killer" Alaki.'

I raised my hands up as some of the crowd cheered for me.

'And fighting out of the red corner, the champion, trained by Jake Carlisle, from Mandurah, Western Australia. Official weight, 90.1 kilograms, standing six feet two inches, tonight wearing the black shorts with red trim, he has defended his title five times. With a professional fight record of forty-seven fights, forty-five wins with fifteen by way of knockout, the Australian favourite and champion in four weight divisions, and the current heavyweight champion – "Golden" Jeff Wilkie.'

Wilkie jumped on the ropes to great cheers and applause, waving his championship belt in the air. At the same time, a girl in a bikini walked into the ring with a sign, announcing the first round of the fight.

The referee called us both into the centre of the ring to make sure we were ready to begin. 'We went over the rules in the change rooms, so these things are not new to you. Fight with the spirit of professional sportsmen. Obey what I say, protect yourselves at all times, keep your punches above the waist at all times. Have a clean fight, good luck to both of you. Touch gloves and go back to your corners.'

We did as we were instructed.

The bell rang and I was fighting for the Australian heavyweight championship.

The fight started equally. My opponent attacked and did everything by the book. It was a slugfest and equally matched after five rounds. The crowd was still yelling but the energy had changed. This fight could be anyone's and the tension ramped up because of that. By the end of the sixth, things were changing. Wilkie had used up all the fuel in his system and it was up to me to show him what my brother taught me. Head straight, back straight, left hand strong, right hand strong and then jab-jab-duck. I started to throw Wilkie off-balance. I was like a machine. My fists were moving so fast he could hardly see them coming his way. The seventh round ended with Wilkie on the ropes until the referee came to separate us.

'Go back to your corner,' the referee said as he helped Wilkie off the ropes.

I went to sit down and could see Vince was already celebrating the victory before the fight was even over.

'Okay, it looks like you've got this one, but you have to stay focused. He's slow now, knock him out in the next round,' Tim said. He was holding the ropes for Lucy to come through. 'Hold the dream, Isa, hold the dream,' Lucy said. 'Don't lose sight of what we set out to do. Hold the dream. It's so close now. Can you see it?'

What I saw was my brother Moïse, back in the schoolyard instructing me and cheering me on. *Come on, Isa, back straight, head up, you gotta kill this kid! Don't be a coward! Finish him off already. Jab, jab, duck!*

The bell went off and I was back in the ring. My hands were up and my head straight. I started doing the moves my brother taught me. I threw a combo of jabs and uppercuts. Powerful body punches. Wilkie was struggling to stay on his feet. As soon as he recovered, I followed up with more pressure. His left eye was closing. Swollen. His face was dripping blood. I was moving around and cutting off the ring. Lucy and Tim were screaming. The crowd was cheering wildly, chanting *'Kill-er! Kill-er!'* over and over. Then I saw Matete walk into the school playground with the whole rebel group. All of them holding weapons, which they waved in the air. Some with their AK-47s and others with machetes.

Sun past point midpoint.

I am walking down the track.

1400 hours.

I'm creeping through green grass.

Angry birds singing uncontrollably.

The husband is floating over a pool of red water.

The young woman, terrified as she clutches her baby to her chest.

Kadogo doesn't stop screaming;

'Do it! Do it now! We are the same, you and I. You can do it. Don't be a coward! Do it!'

The baby frees himself from the hands of his dead mother. Stains of blood splash on the baby's face, dripping down his small neck to his shirt. His crying voice is distinguishable from everything else around us. Kadogo has his gun on my brother's forehead. I hold a rock in my hand, the size of a pawaw. My brother looks at me momentarily, then crash-tackles Kadogo.

'Run! Run, Isa!' He screams louder than anyone else. 'Run!'

I drop my AK-47 and start to run. Weaving and ducking past the bushes through smoke and sounds of trumpets in the distance. As I continue running,

I hear two gunshots. I stop to look back. Now, I can clearly see them both. Kadogo, with his hand pressing his stomach; he's wounded from the gunshots my brother fired at him. He stumbles and waves his gun and points it at Moïse. Moïse stands there, defiantly, yelling the words 'Run, Isa!' as he stares Kadogo down. Kadogo fires. He strikes Moïse in the chest twice. As my brother falls to the ground he releases another barrage of gunshots, blasting at least half a magazine into Kadogo's body. I turn and run and run and run.

The sound of the roaring crowd brought me back. The referee raised his hand.

Lucy, Tim and two paramedics rushed into the ring to help me.

I woke up in the hospital with Lucy, Tim and Trinity at my bedside.

'What happened?' I asked.

'You fainted,' Lucy said. 'Right when you were about to win the fight. But you made us proud,' she said. 'You're a true champion, Isa. I know you'll be fine. Take some time off. Do whatever you gotta to do. Vince wasn't happy but the rematch will make a fortune!'

After Tim and Lucy left, Trinity stayed with me. She sat silently by my bed and I lay there, staring at the ceiling of the hospital room. Moïse was dead. I knew that now. I think I'd always known it. But my mind couldn't cope with that devastating truth. Moïse had given his life to save me.

Trinity held me as I cried, and I told her what I now knew was the truth.

A few days later, after scans and assessments, I was released from hospital. I didn't know exactly what I was going to do but I started to run. I liked the rhythm of my feet hitting the ground, the way it connected me to the earth and to the family that had been – and would always be – part of me. It was up to me to take the Alaki name and make my father proud. To start the Bembe tribe in this new, safe place.

I would do what my father had wanted for his children. I would have a better life.

ACT V

chapter 22

forgiveness doesn't
need a ransom

AFTER A MONTH, WHEN I HAD FULLY RECOVERED, I
booked a flight back to the DRC. I put my brother's
slingshot in my backpack and headed to my old home.
After three days of flights from Brisbane to Kigoma,
and a boat ride from there, I arrived at the shore of Lake
Tanganyika in Uvira. I was meeting Trésor Mbanu there,
the private investigator, but the guards who wanted to
see my pass stopped me. When I took out my Australian
passport, they were very attentive. They asked me why I
lived in Australia when I was born in the DRC.

'You are a traitor,' one guard said. 'We are going to
report you to the army's Commander in Chief.'

I was forced to wait in a small room. I knew how to do
that. I was interviewed and was there for an hour before

Trésor Mbanu found me. I don't know how he knew to come to that place but I was very glad he did.

Trésor identified me as the son of the man who was about to bring change, and after convincing their commander, I was allowed to leave. But only after a crate of beer and a pack of cigarettes had changed hands.

'My condolences for your loss,' he said as we walked out of the building to a waiting car. He had arranged for three of his best security agents to guard me while I was in the country. My old home was still a dangerous place.

We travelled by car along a dusty potholed road, past abandoned villages and rusty vehicles. Some of the buildings were still standing from the time of the Belgians but they were decayed. From time to time, I saw glimpses of what it had been like when I lived there. But then we passed three trucks filled with government soldiers and more on foot, marching out on one of their murderous rampages.

'They are getting ready for an attack,' one of the guards said. 'There have been rumours of rebel activities in the region.'

'How bad is it?' I asked.

'War will never end in the DRC,' Trésor said. 'As long as those minerals still lie beneath our feet, someone will always find a reason to start another war over them. More men, women and children have died here than those who lost their lives in the Holocaust, but there is no mention in the media about what's happening here. All because the rest of the world depends on our resources.'

His words replayed in the back of my mind like an alarm on snooze as we drove onto an endless road towards the village where I last saw Moïse.

'This is a hell road,' Trésor said. 'More people have died on this road than you can think of. When the Banyamulenge came in, they killed a lot of people who were escaping. We came and buried thousands into one big mass grave.' He showed me a large cemented grave by the roadside. 'We buried all of the people Banyamulenge killed in here. Men, women and children. They didn't care if you were a child or not. Slaughtered all of them like animals. The sight was horrendous.' He went quiet for a while. 'This is a hell road,' he repeated.

We were all silent after that.

Finally, we entered the village near where I had last seen my brother. We passed the hill at the beginning of the village. The same hill that Kadogo, Moïse, Delta Force and I were supposed to go to plant a cannon.

'Can we go to the hill?' I asked.

'You have to ask the village elders for permission first,' Trésor said.

We went to find the village leader and asked for permission to visit the stream. He lived in a small mud house in the middle of the village with his wife. Mr Mbuyu they called him. He walked with us to the stream where my brother and I saw the young couple who were escaping. I stood looking up at the hill, by the bank of the river.

'Matete attacked our village,' Mr Mbuyu said. 'A lot of people died that day. We buried them all. I was here that day and helped gather the bodies. Where we are standing, I found two of Matete's men dead and the body of a young woman. Her child was cuddled up to her chest.'

I did not know if I had the strength to speak and reveal what I knew.

'Where did you bury them?' I asked. My throat was dry.

Mr Mbuyu showed me a spot a little away from the riverbank. 'We found the little boy's relatives; he lives with his grandfather now. His father's body was never found.'

I stood silently on the place my brother was buried. I asked for a moment, and the others walked away. I took Moïse's slingshot out of the backpack I carried and I crouched down and dug a hole. I placed Moïse's slingshot in the hole and covered it with the earth. The same earth that held Moïse, my father, my mother and Rita. The land that cradled their souls and the land that would always be a part of me. I broke down in tears. Sobbing inconsolably.

As Mr Mbuyu walked back over to me I said, 'Those two boys you found dead here, one of them was my older brother,' I said. 'I was here when it happened. He died protecting the little boy. Can I visit the boy?'

'I think so,' Mr Mbuyu said. 'Let me talk to the family.'

It felt like I had released the heaviest thing I had been carrying for a long time. I stayed there, crying for almost half an hour before Mr Mbuyu insisted that we leave. We made our way back to the village to find the boy, who was now eleven. A year older than I was when I became a child soldier. He was living in a small baked-mud house with a galvanised roof. Three other small houses surrounded the compound with the main road close to it. I saw a young boy playing with his friends when we got to the house. Mr Mbuyu asked me to wait and he walked over to an old man cutting a pile of sugarcane with a big machete.

Ékolo'yo; Mr Mbuyu greeted the old man in my dialect.

Ékolo'yo; the old man responded.

'I brought with me this young man,' he gestured towards me. 'He wanted to come and see Tumaini.'

'Where did he come from?' the old man asked.

'He's come from a long way,' Mr Mbuyu continued, responding in my dialect.

The old man brought two long benches from his house and gestured for us to sit. Trésor, Mr Mbuyu and I sat on one bench and the three guards sat on the other.

'This is the father of the woman who is now in the grave we were at,' Mr Mbuyu said.

I took my backpack and put it on the floor as I went down on my knees in front of the old man.

'I was there when your daughter died,' I said. 'I was there when a boy I knew gunned down your son-in-law. He died in the river when he was trying to flee with your daughter and grandson. My brother saved your grandson's life, but these are the hands that took your daughter's.' I held up my hands, tears rolling down my face.

The old man looked at me for a long time. Then he took a few steps towards me and folded his arms around me in a hug. Tears rolled down his face when he held me. 'From the very bottom of my heart I forgive you,' the old man said. 'There has been too much war and too much anger.

We cannot heal if we carry that with us. Bring the boy for me,' he called to his wife. Soon after, the boy appeared. Barefoot with an old tattered shirt and too-small shorts.

'This is Tumaini,' the old man said. 'His name means "hope".' The young boy ran into his grandpa's embrace. 'He's our hope. A boy who escapes such a horrendous battle is a warrior. That's why we call him Tumaini.'

'How are you, Tumaini?' I asked.

'Good,' he responded. 'Most people call me "Tuma".'

'My name is Isa. I have a gift for you.' I reached down into my pocket to take out two thousand dollars and handed it over to the old man. 'I know this cannot repay your loss, but I want you to keep it,' I said.

'Forgiveness doesn't need a ransom,' the old man said.

'It's a gift for Tuma,' I insisted.

After a meal, it was time to leave. Trésor drove us back to Bukavu: there was one more place I needed to go. We went to my street, the place I had watched my whole family massacred. I was nervous to approach our house. A heavily burnt LandCruiser was sitting on the side of the road, where children were playing hide and seek. The gate to our home was broken and leaning, and in place of my mother's beautiful garden was a pumpkin patch. A young couple now lived in our house; they told me they bought the place from the government. I walked over to where I knew my parents and my sister's bodies lay. The only thing that showed the ground had been disturbed was an indentation, the earth not quite level. I stood there not sure what to do and then asked Tresor where I could buy some crosses and some cement. For fewer than five hundred dollars, I paid men to embed three crosses in the ground above where the bones of my family lay. At last, their graves were marked. I felt that this would give them peace. But maybe it was just me who finally had some peace.

It was time for me to go back home to Australia to work on myself, work on my ambitions and achieve my dreams.

I took a boat back to Kigoma and then took a flight to Dar es Salaam before boarding my flight to Brisbane.

I looked out the window as the plane circled over Moreton Bay to prepare to land. It looked like diamonds lay in a thick line across the water, sparkling in the early morning light. So different to where I'd come from.

As I went through Customs the officer asked me my name. I smiled.

'My name is Isa Alaki, and I am from here.'

acknowledgements

Hoshikyo suyâ, asona oheta wa lohimo
'A person who doesn't appreciate is worse
than a stingy one'
BEMBE PROVERB

Prize Fighter is special to me, as much as it is to many other people who have had similar experiences, or more, than I have. But I cannot say that this was a journey that I took on my own. Of course, there are many people that helped me along the way.

First of all, I want to thank the Almighty God for opening the doors that lead me to this chapter. I will never stop thanking Him for everything he's done for me in my life.

God bless my family who have always been there and made sure that I had a full stomach while I was writing the play that made it to the stage and then into this book. My sister Okanya Safi, younger brother Mike – along with his wife Josephine – and my younger sister Gloria. I want to thank the Yukepi family for their consistent prayers.

Next, in no particular order, I want to thank Roger Monk and Emily Avila for their contribution to the work; Jackie McKimmie and her husband Chris; Gypsey Marva for her everyday motivation; Chris Kohn for believing in the story of *Prize Fighter* and giving it a chance to see the light of day. I also want to thank Michael Futcher for guiding me along the way.

The staff at La Boite Theatre Company, past and present. Those who did everything possible to make the work a special one: Todd MacDonald, Nicholas Paine, Glyn Roberts, Rhys Holden, David Berthold. You never stopped believing in the work and went the extra mile to make sure it was noticed in such big programs as the Brisbane Festival and Sydney Festival.

Special thanks to Pacharo Mzembe who gave it his all to make sure that the story was told the way it was intended to be.

And last but certainly not the least, I want to thank my publisher, Vanessa Radnidge, for making the decision to bring this story to the page, and for believing that it was not just a story, but a life-changing journey that readers will now get to experience.

hachette
AUSTRALIA

If you would like to find out more about Hachette Australia,
our authors, upcoming events and new releases you can
visit our website or our social media channels:

hachette.com.au
f HachetteAustralia
🐦 📷 👻 HachetteAus